PENGUIN BOOKS

THE FRIENDS OF EDDIE COYLE

George V. Higgins was formerly an Assistant U.S. Attorney for the District of Massachusetts. Born in Brockton, Massachusetts, in 1939, he was graduated from Boston College and received an M.A. in English from Stanford University. He was a reporter for the Providence *Journal* and the Associated Press before obtaining a law degree from Boston College Law School in 1967. For three years he was a lawyer in the Massachusetts Attorney General's office, in the Organized Crime Section and the Criminal Division. Mr. Higgins has contributed articles to legal journals, published short stories in *Arizona Quarterly*, *The Massachusetts Review*, and *North American Review*, and written book reviews for the Boston *Herald-Traveler*. The author of numerous novels as well as several books of nonfiction, he lives in Milton, Massachusetts.

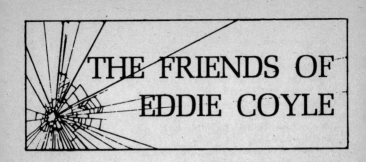

THE FRIENDS OF
EDDIE COYLE

George V. Higgins

PENGUIN BOOKS

PENGUIN BOOKS
Viking Penguin Inc., 40 West 23rd Street,
New York, New York 10010, U.S.A.
Penguin Books Ltd, Harmondsworth,
Middlesex, England
Penguin Books Australia Ltd, Ringwood,
Victoria, Australia
Penguin Books Canada Limited, 2801 John Street,
Markham, Ontario, Canada L3R 1B4
Penguin Books (N.Z.) Ltd, 182–190 Wairau Road,
Auckland 10, New Zealand

First published in the United States of America by
Alfred A. Knopf, Inc., 1971
Reprinted by arrangement with Alfred A. Knopf, Inc.
Published in Penguin Books 1987

LIBRARY OF CONGRESS CATALOGING IN PUBLICATION DATA
Higgins, George V.
    The friends of Eddie Coyle.
    I. Title.
PS3558.I356F7 1987   813′.54   86-30399
ISBN 0 14 01.0232 9

A part of Chapter 6 appeared in a different form under the title
"Dillon Explained That He Was Frightened" in *North American
Review*, Fall, 1970.

Printed in the United States of America by
Offset Paperback Mfrs., Inc., Dallas, Pennsylvania
Set in Caledonia

THE FRIENDS OF EDDIE COYLE

JACKIE BROWN at twenty-six, with no expression on his face, said that he could get some guns. "I can get your pieces probably by tomorrow night. I can get you, probably, six pieces. Tomorrow night. In a week or so, maybe ten days, another dozen. I got a guy coming in with at least ten of them but I already talk to another guy about four of them and he's, you know, expecting them. He's got something to do. So, six tomorrow night. Another dozen in a week."

The stocky man sat across from Jackie Brown and allowed his coffee to grow cold. "I don't know as I like that," he said. "I don't know as I like buying stuff from the same lot as somebody else. Like, I don't know what he's going to do with it, you know? If it was to cause trouble to my people on account of somebody else having some from the same lot, well, it could cause trouble for me, too."

"I understand," Jackie Brown said. People who got out early from work went by in the November afternoon, hurrying. The crippled man hawked *Records*, annoying people by crying at them from his skate-wheeled dolly.

"You don't understand the way I understand," the stocky man said. "I got certain responsibilities."

"Look," Jackie Brown said, "I tell you I understand. Did you get my name or didn't you?"

"I got your name," the stocky man said.

"Well all right," Jackie Brown said.

"All right nothing," the stocky man said. "I wished I

had a nickel for every name I got that was all right, I wished I did. Look at this." The stocky man extended the fingers of his left hand over the gold-speckled formica tabletop. "You know what that is?"

"Your hand," Jackie Brown said.

"I hope you look closer at guns'n you look at that hand," the stocky man said. "Look at your own goddamned hand."

Jackie Brown extended the fingers of his left hand. "Yeah," he said.

"Count your fucking knuckles," the stocky man said.

"All of them?" Jackie Brown said.

"Ah Christ," the stocky man said. "Count as many of them as you want. I got four more. One on each finger. Know how I got those? I bought some stuff from a man that I had his name, and it got traced, and the man I bought it for, he went to M C I Walpole for fifteen to twenty-five. Still in there, but he had some friends. I got an extra set of knuckles. Shut my hand in a drawer. Then one of them stomped the drawer shut. Hurt like a fucking bastard. You got no idea how it hurt."

"Jesus," Jackie Brown said.

"What made it hurt more," the stocky man said, "what made it hurt worse was knowing what they were going to do to you, you know? There you are and they tell you very matter of fact that you made somebody mad, you made a big mistake and now there's somebody doing time for it, and it isn't anything personal, you understand, but it just has to be done. Now get your hand out there. You think about not doing it, you know? I was in Sunday School when I was a kid and this nun says to me, stick out your hand, and the first few times I do it she whacks me right across the knuckles with a steel-edged ruler. It was just like that. So one day I says, when she tells me 'Put out your hand,' I say, 'No.' And she whaps me right across the face with that ruler. Same thing. Except these guys weren't mad, they aren't mad at you, you know? Guys you see all the time, maybe guys you didn't like, maybe guys you did, had some drinks with, maybe looked out for the girls. 'Hey look, Paulie, nothing personal, you know? You made a mistake. The hand. I don't wanna have to *shoot* you, you know.' So you stick out the hand and — you get to put out the hand you want — I take the left because I'm right-handed and I know what's going to happen, like I say, and they put your fingers in the drawer and then one of them kicks it shut. Ever hear bones breaking? Just like a man snapping a shingle. Hurts like a bastard."

"Jesus," Jackie Brown said.

"That's what I mean," the stocky man said. "I had a cast on for almost a month. Weather gets damp, it still hurts. I can't bend them fingers. So I don't care what your name is, who gave it to me. I had the other guy's name, and that didn't help my goddamn fingers. Name isn't enough. I get paid for being careful. What I want to know is, what happens one of the other guns from this bunch gets traced? Am I going to have to start pricing crutches? This is serious business, you know. I don't know who you been selling to before, but the fellow says you got guns to sell and I need guns. I'm just protecting myself, just being smart. What happens when the man with the four gives one to somebody that uses it to shoot a goddamned cop? I gotta leave town?"

"No," Jackie Brown said.

"No?" the stocky man said. "Okay, I hope you're right about that. I'm running short of fingers. And if I gotta leave town, my friend, you gotta leave town. You understand that. They'll do it to me, they'll do worse to you. You know that."

"I know that," Jackie Brown said.

"I hope you do," the stocky man said. "I dunno who you been selling to, but I can tell you, these guys're different."

"You can't trace these guns," Jackie Brown said. "I guarantee it."

"Tell me how come," the stocky man said.

"Look," Jackie Brown said, "these're new guns, follow me? Proof, test-firing's all they ever had. Brand-fucking-new guns. Airweights. Shrouded hammers. Floating firing pins. You could drop one of these pieces right on the hammer with a round in the chamber — nothing. Thirty-eight Specials. I'm telling you, it's good stuff."

"Stolen," the stocky man said. "Serial numbers filed off. That's how I got caught before. They got this bath they drop the stuff in, raises that number right back again. You better do better'n that, neither one of us'll be able to shake hands."

"No," Jackie Brown said. "They got serial numbers. Man gets caught with one of them, perfectly all right, no sweat. No way to tell it's stolen. Brand-new gun."

"With a serial number?" the stocky man said.

"You look up the serial number," Jackie Brown said, "it's a Military Police model, made in 1951, shipped to Rock Island, never reported stolen. But it's a brand-new Detective Special. Never reported stolen either."

"You got somebody in the plant," the stocky man said.

"I got guns to sell," Jackie Brown said. "I done a lot of business and I had very few complaints. I can get you four-inchers and two-inchers. You just tell me what you want. I can deliver it."

"How much?" the stocky man said.

"Depends on the lot," Jackie Brown said.

"Depends on what I'm willing to pay, too," the stocky man said. "How much?"

"Eighty," Jackie Brown said.

"Eighty?" the stocky man said. "You ever sell guns before? Eighty is way too high. I'm talking about thirty guns here now. I can go into a goddamned *store* and buy thirty guns for eighty apiece. We got to talk some more about price, I can see that."

"I'd like to see you go into a store and order up thirty pieces," Jackie Brown said. "I don't know who you are and I don't know what you got in mind and I don't need to know. But I would sure like to be there when you tell the man you got some friends in the market for thirty pieces and you want a discount. I would like to see that. The FBI'd be onto your phone before you got the money out."

"There's more'n one gun store, you know," the stocky man said.

"Not for you there isn't," Jackie Brown said. "I can tell you right now there isn't anybody for a hundred miles that can put up the goods like I can, and you know it. So no more of that shit."

"I never went over fifty before," the stocky man said. "I'm not going that high now. You haven't got that many guys around waiting to take thirty, either. And if these work out all right, I'll be coming back for more. You're used to dealing in twos and threes, that's why you want to deliver three or four times."

"I can sell fifty tomorrow without ever seeing you," Jackie Brown said. "I can't get my hands on them fast enough. I can sell every gun I can get. I bet if I was to go down to the Shrine there and go to confession I'd get three Hail Marys and the priest'd ask me confidentially if I could get him something light he could carry under his coat. People're desperate for guns. I had a guy last week that was hot for a Python and I got him this big fucking Blackhawk, six-incher, forty-one mag, and he took it like he'd been looking for it all his life. Should've seen that bastard going out, big lump under his coat, looked like he was stealing melons. I had a guy seriously ask me, could I get him a few machineguns. He'd go a buck and a half apiece for as many as I could get, didn't even care what caliber."

"What color was he?" the stocky man asked.

"He was a nice fellow," Jackie Brown said. "I wouldn't be surprised if I was to be able to get something for him in a week or so. Good material, too. M-sixteens in very nice shape."

"I never been able to understand a man that wanted to use a machinegun," the stocky man said. "It's life if you get hooked with it and you can't really do much of anything with it except fight a war, maybe. You can't hide it and you can't carry it around in a car and you can't hit anything with the goddamned thing unless you don't mind shooting out a couple of walls getting the guy. Which is risky. I don't care much for a machinegun. The best all-around item I ever saw is the four-inch Smith. Now that is a fine piece of machinery, you can heft it and it goes where you point it."

"It's too big for a lot of people," Jackie Brown said. "I had a man that wanted a couple of thirty-eights a week or so ago, and I come up with one of those and a Colt two-incher. He liked the Colt all right but he was all edgy about the Smith. Asked me if I thought he was going to go around wearing a fucking holster or something. But he took it just the same."

"Look," the stocky man said, "I want thirty guns. I'll take four-inchers and two-inchers. Thirty-eights, I'll take a three-fifty-seven mag if I have to. Thirty pieces. I'll give you twelve hundred."

"Balls," Jackie Brown said. "I got to have at least seventy apiece."

"I'll go fifteen hundred," the stocky man said.

"Split the difference," Jackie Brown said. "Eighteen hundred."

"I'll have to see the stuff," the stocky man said.

"Sure," Jackie Brown said. His expression changed: he smiled.

2

THE STRAWBERRY ice cream soda and the dark green Charger R/T arrived in the stocky man's vision almost simultaneously. The waitress went away and he watched the car travel slowly past the stores and stop at the far end of the parking lot. He unwrapped the plastic straw and began without haste to drink the soda. The driver of the car remained inside.

The stocky man paid for his soda and said to the waitress: "I was wondering if there was a men's room here." She gestured toward the back of the store. The stocky man walked into the narrow corridor at the rear, past the rest rooms. Beyond him there was a screen door ajar on a loading platform. He went out on the loading platform and crouched. He jumped clumsily off the platform onto the service road. Two hundred yards away there was another loading platform. When he reached it, he clambered up and entered through a metal door marked PRODUCE ONLY. Inside there was a young man sorting lettuce. The stocky man offered an explanation: "My car broke down out on the street there. Is there a phone in here I can use?" The young man said something about a phone near the registers in front. The stocky man left the store by the front door. He took a general view of the parking lot. When his vision settled on the Charger he began to walk toward it.

The driver unlocked the passenger door of the

Charger and the stocky man got in. The stocky man said: "Been waiting long?"

The driver was about thirty-five. He was wearing suede boots, flared tweed slacks, a gold turtleneck sweater and a glossy black leather car coat. He had long hair and wore broad sunglasses with heavy silver frames. "As long as it took you to decide it was safe to come out," he said. "What the hell made you choose this place? You getting your hair done or something?"

"I heard they were having a special on skis," the stocky man said. "This is a pretty nice car you got here. Anybody I know?"

"I don't think so," the driver said. "Fellow out in the western part of the state was using it to transport moon. Poor bastard. Paid cash for it and got hooked on his first trip. I don't see how the hell they can afford to sell the stuff when they got to buy a new car every time they take a load out."

"Sometimes they get away with it," the stocky man said.

"I didn't know that was in your line," the driver said.

"Well, it isn't," the stocky man said, "but you hear things from time to time, you know. People're careless."

"I know," the driver said. "Like last week I heard you were coming up for disposition in New Hampshire the fifteenth of January, and I said to myself, I wonder where Eddie's got plans to spend the Fourth of July."

"That's why I was interested in the skis," the stocky man said. "I figure as long as I got to go up there I might as well make a weekend out of it, you know? Think we'll have snow by then?"

"I think we're getting some right now," the driver said.

"Because I was thinking, if we did," the stocky man said, "maybe you could join me for the weekend. You'd make out like a bandit, those clothes, the car."

"Then on Tuesday we could drive down to court together," the driver said.

"That's right," the stocky man said. "Make a nice outing. Give you a chance to say hello to all your old friends up there. What the hell're you chasing now, queers?"

"They got me on drugs," the driver said. "So far all I got is pot, but they tell me there's some hash floating around in the real swinging places, and they borrowed me to look for it."

The stocky man said: "But you're still interested in machineguns, I suppose."

"Yes indeed," the driver said. "I always had a strong interest in a machinegun or two."

"That's what I was thinking," the stocky man said. "I said to myself, Old Dave is reliable. I wonder what he's doing now, if he remembers his old friends and the machineguns. That's why I looked you up."

"Just what old friends, for example?" the driver said.

"Well, I was thinking, for example," the stocky man said, "maybe the U.S. Attorney up there. He's an old friend of yours, as I recall."

"You thought I might enjoy a chance to talk with him," the driver said.

"I figured it was worth asking," the stocky man said.

"That's an awful long way to go to see somebody I can talk to on the phone," the driver said. "Still, if I had a strong reason."

"Well," the stocky man said, "I got three kids and a

wife at home, and I can't afford to do no more time, you know? The kids're growing up and they go to school and the other kids make fun of them and all. Hell, I'm almost forty-five years old."

"That's your strong reason," the driver said. "I need one for me. What're they holding over you, about five years?"

"My lawyer guesses about two or so," the stocky man said.

"You'll do well to get out with two," the driver said. "You had about two hundred cases of C.C. on that truck, way I remember it, and none of it belonged to you. Belonged to a fellow up in Burlington, I think it was, and you made a mistake like that before."

"I keep telling you," the stocky man said, "it was all a mistake. I was minding my own business and getting along the best I could and this fellow called me up, knew I was out of work, and he asks me, would I drive a truck for him? That's all there was to it. I didn't know that guy from Burlington from Adam."

"I can see how that could happen," the driver said. "Man like you lives in Wrentham, Massachusetts, must get a lot of calls to drive a semi from Burlington to Portland, especially when I never heard of you making a living driving a truck before. I can see how that could happen. I'm surprised the jury didn't believe you."

"My stupid lawyer," the stocky man said. "He's not as smart as you. Wouldn't let me take the stand and tell them how it happened. They never heard the whole story."

"Why don't you appeal on that?" the driver said.

"I thought about it," the stocky man said. "Incompe-

tence of counsel. I knew a fellow got out on that one.
Trouble is, I haven't got time to write up the papers. I
know where there's a guy that does it, but he's down in
Danbury I think, and I don't want to see him particularly. Anyway, I was wondering if maybe there wasn't
an easier way of handling it."

"Like me saying hello to somebody," the driver said.

"Actually, something a little stronger than that," the
stocky man said. "I was thinking more in terms of you
having the prosecutor tell the judge how I been helping
my uncle like a bastard."

"Well, I would," the driver said. "But then again, you
haven't been. We're old buddies and all, Eddie, but I
got to take Scout's Honor when I do that. And what
am I going to tell them about you? That you were instrumental in recovering two hundred cases of Canadian
Club? I don't think that's going to help you much."

"I called you a few times," the stocky man said.

"You gave me some real stuff, too," the driver said.
"You tell me about a guy that's going to get hit and
fifteen minutes later he gets hit. You tell me about
some fellows that're planning a bank job, but you don't
get around to telling me until they're coming out the
door with the money and everybody in the world
knows about it. That's not working for uncle, Eddie.
You got to put your whole soul into it. Hell, I been
hearing it around that maybe you're not even really
going straight. I keep hearing you're maybe mixed up
in something else that's going on."

"Like what?" the stocky man said.

"Oh, well," the driver said, "you know how it is with
what you hear. I wouldn't confront a man with something I heard. You know me better'n that."

"Well," the stocky man said, "suppose we were to talk about some machineguns."

"Just to change the subject," the driver said.

"Yeah," the stocky man said. "Suppose you had a reliable informer that put you onto a colored gentleman that was buying some machineguns. Army machineguns, M-sixteens. Would you want a fellow like that, that was helping you like that, would you want him to go to jail and embarrass his kids and all?"

"Let me put it this way," the agent said, "if I was to get my hands on the machineguns *and* the colored gentleman *and* the fellow that was selling the machineguns, and if that happened because somebody put me in the right place at the right time with maybe a warrant, I wouldn't mind saying to somebody else that the fellow who put me there was helping uncle. Does the colored gentleman have any friends?"

"I wouldn't be surprised," the stocky man said. "Thing is, I just found out about it yesterday."

"How'd you find out?" the driver said.

"Well, one thing and another," the stocky man said. "You know how it is, you're talking to somebody and he says something and the next fellow says something, and the first thing you know, you heard something."

"When's it supposed to come off?" the driver said.

"I'm not sure yet," the stocky man said. "See, I'm right on the button with this one, I come to you soon as I heard it. I got more things to find out, if you're — if you think you might be interested. I think a week or so. Why don't I call you?"

"Okay," the driver said. "Do you need anything else?"

"I need a good leaving alone," the stocky man said.

"I'd as soon not have anybody start thinking about me too much on this detail. I don't want nobody following me around, all right?"

"Okay," the driver said, "we'll do it your way. You call me when you get something, if you do, and if I get something, I'll put it in front of the U.S. Attorney. If I don't, all bets're off. Understood?"

The stocky man nodded.

"Merry Christmas," the driver said.

3

THREE HEAVYSET men wearing nylon windbreakers and plaid woolen shirts, each of them holding a can of Schaefer beer, marched past the stocky man under Gate A as the first quarter ended. One of the men said: "I don't know why the fuck I come down here every week, I don't know the fuck why I do. Look at those stupid bastards, fifteen minutes, down seventeen points, Buffalo's running right through them. It was nine points on the card and I took the Pats because I figure they'll at least stay that close. Goddamned game."

Several minutes later a man with a florid complexion, his face scarred from acne, came up to the stocky man. "You take your own fucking time showing up, don't you?" the stocky man said.

"Look," the second man said. "I get up this morning and take the kids to church and the little bastards screamed so bad I had to take them out. Then the old lady starts the music about how I never stay home, and I won't finish painting the house and the car's all goddamned dirty and everything else. I couldn't find a place to park when I got here. So why don't you shut your goddamned mouth, I had enough people yakking at me today."

"It's a shitty game anyway," the stocky man said.

"I know," the second man said, "I heard it on the radio coming in. It was ten to nothing when I left the car."

"It's seventeen now," the stocky man said. "They still

haven't scored. I was talking to Dillon the other day at his place and I was saying to him, has somebody got something in with them. And he says no, what the hell is there to fix? They don't have a good enough defense to hold the other side down, and they don't have any offense to run their own up, so what the hell is there to do?"

"I heard something about Dillon that I didn't like," the second man said.

"I know it," the stocky man said. "I heard that too."

"See, he was with Arthur and the Polack that night, and I hear something about a grand jury. Which I don't like a bit."

"Well," the stocky man said, "you got nothing to worry about. You didn't have anything to do with that."

"Never mind what I had to do with it," the second man said. "I don't like to see them getting close to Arthur. Next time he goes it'll be two-thirds mandatory, at least, and Arthur does hard time. He gets to thinking too much. When he was in Billerica the last time there, a couple of us had to go up and see him and cheer him up once, twice. One of the screws saw him getting chummy with the chaplain up there, which is usually the tip-off with Arthur. He damned near got in trouble when Lewis got grabbed with those stocks that time, but they couldn't be sure he did it."

"Arthur's a good man," the stocky man said.

"Arthur's as tight as a popcorn fart when he's on a job," the second man said, "but you sit him away some place where he's got too much time to think and he's dangerous. He'd fuck a dog with scarlet fever to get parole."

"Well, you know him better'n I do," the stocky man said. "I always liked him."

"You can't beat him on a job," the second man said. "No question about that. I wouldn't go for this thing if Arthur wasn't on it. You get in somewhere and somebody starts getting nervous, some woman teller or something, and everybody's all lathered up anyway, you got to have Arthur along. I never heard a shot fired when Arthur's in there. He tells somebody he'll shoot them if they don't do what he says, they always do it. They believe Arthur. He looks like he means what he says, so you don't have to do anything. It's afterwards that you got to worry about Arthur, and you don't have to then unless he gets in the slam for something. It's a risk you got to take."

"I think I got the guns you want," the stocky man said.

"They look pretty good, do they?" the second man said.

"Well, they oughta," the stocky man said. "I hadda go seventy apiece for them. Yeah, they look good. Brand-new."

"I like that," the second man said. "I don't like walking around with no gun that I don't know where it's been before. You can't tell what'll happen, you go in on a simple job and something goes wrong and you figure, shit, seven to ten at least, depending on who's sitting, and the next thing you know they traced the goddamned thing back to some guy that used it on a hit and you got an accessory-after hanging over you. It's dangerous enough as it is without taking that kind of a chance."

"That's what I figured," the stocky man said. "Ordinarily, I don't like to go that high, but I figured, well, if it's good stuff it's probably worth the money. There's so much shit around, you know? Guy was telling me, he was talking to this nigger about a warehouse he'd been looking at. See, it was in the jungle there and he was looking for somebody that could sit in a car without looking like he didn't belong there, you know? Straight cash, a hundred bucks to sit in the car, thousand if they got what they went after. Couldn't miss, he was saying, color tee-vees, sewing machines, portable stereos, that kind of thing. Real good stuff, move it fast. So he tells this big coon he'll have to have a gun and the guy says, all right, I know where I can get a pretty good piece.

"So they pick him up and they're on the way to get the truck and so forth, and the guy tells me he says to him: 'Oh by the way, you got yourself a gun, I suppose.' And the nigger says sure, and he pulls out this shopping bag, and what has he got in there but one of those German Mausers, machinepistol, remember the kind that had that wooden holster that you could put on and use it like a rifle? Beautiful thing. So they're all very impressed and they're riding along on the Lynnway, I guess it was, and anyway the guy says to him, well, is it loaded? And the jig says, no, he's going to load it right there. So he comes up with this clip and he snaps it in and that whole clip went, barrap, just like that, something like a handful of nine-millimeters flying around in the car and people practically jumping out of windows. So they hadda call off the job, of course, and get rid of the car. Nobody got hurt, but the next day the guy goes back again to look at the warehouse and there're the distributor's trucks pulled up outside. 'I never been so pissed off in my life,' he says to me. 'You know what they got in there now? They got blankets. Tons and tons of fucking blankets, and I coulda had a million bucks worth of tee-vees if it wasn't for that stupid nigger and his goddamned gun. Never trust a goddamned nigger,' he says, 'never trust them, that's all. They'll fuck you up every time.' "

"I don't like an automatic," the second man said. "I had one once and I pulled it out and pointed it at the guy and good thing for me, he backed down. Then I think, well, as long as I got it out I might as well check it out, and I didn't have one in the chamber. You can't tell with one of those things. If he'd've come at me I would've stood there dry-snapping it at him and he'd've taken my fucking head off. You just don't have time to crank one in when you need a piece, is all, and I never met a guy yet that used one regular and didn't get himself in some kind of a close one, sooner or later, on account of the fucking thing jamming on him when he needed it. I like a goddamned revolver."

"I got what you want, then," the stocky man said. "I got eight of them. Five Smiths, a Colt Python and two Rugers. Forty-one mags, the Rugers. That fucking mag looks just like a cannon, so help me. Got a mouth on her like the Sumner Tunnel. You could hold up a bank all by yourself with that thing."

"What're the Smiths?" the second man said. "Thirty-eights, I hope. I don't know as I can get any of that forty-one ammo."

"Three of them're thirty-eights," the stocky man said. "Two three-fifty-sevens, not that it matters. Great big ventilated ribs on the mags. Look, you need shells for anything, I can get you that too."

"I'm all set on thirty-eights, as far as that goes," the second man said. "You could get me some three-fifty-seven and forty-one ammo, I'd appreciate it. What's it all going to cost me?"

"Usual rate," the stocky man said. "Buck and a half for all the guns, every one of them, I mean. I'll throw in the ammo, account you're a good customer and all."

"Twelve bills," the second man said. "Fair enough."

"Okay," the stocky man said. "Now, you still want the rest of the order, don't you? I mean, I got ten more at least, coming early part of next week. And then, well, you said you wanted about thirty, and I figure the rest of them'll be in before, say, the end of the month."

"Oh sure," the second man said. "I can use anything you can get. We're going to need at least five Monday, maybe more, if Arthur decides to get enough people to do the job right. And I like to have a couple extras in the car, you know? So if you got to use one on the job you can wipe it off and heave it down the river and still have something on hand. So if everything goes right, we'll probably be dumping the whole eight you got for me by Monday night, and that'll mean I'll need the next batch fast."

"I got a week, though," the stocky man said.

"Look," the second man said, "unless I can talk Arthur into acting sensible, you probably got a year. That dumb son of a bitch, he won't throw a gun away. Gets attached to them. I don't know how many times I told him to get rid of a piece and he'd say: 'No, I paid a hundred for this gun,' or whatever it was he paid for it, 'and I didn't even use it yet. No reason to throw it away.' And he's sitting there with ten, eleven grand in the pocket. So he gets whipped in three days after the

Lowell job and he's got a gun on him and they don't even have to prove he was on the Lowell thing, they give him a fat three or so for carrying without a permit. And then they laugh at him. He's the tightest son of a bitch I've ever seen. But I think maybe that taught him something. He did, what, twenty months of that for a gun that cost him maybe a hundred bucks. Five dollars a month he saved. You can get electric lights for five bucks a month, and Arthur goes to jail. Dumb fuck. But you figure, I can use the whole thirty probably by Christmas. You go ahead."

"All right," the stocky man said. "When do you want them? It isn't tomorrow, is it?"

"What do you mean?" the second man said. "Oh, no, a week from tomorrow. I'd like to pick them up probably tomorrow."

"Same place?" the stocky man said.

"I think that's going to be a little out of my way tomorrow," the second man said. "I got to be somewhere else. I tell you, I'll give you a call and you come and meet me. When I call you, I'll tell you where I'm going to be."

"I wasn't planning to be home," the stocky man said.

"Okay," the second man said. "What I'll do is call Dillon as soon as I know where I'm going to be and tell him I told my wife I was going to be there, and have him tell her if she calls that I went out but I'm coming back and he'll have me call her. Then for him to call me and tell me she called. I'll leave a number. I'll do that before nine. You call Dillon and tell him you called me at home and my wife said I was at Dillon's, and he won't think anything, he'll give you the number and you can call me up and we'll meet somewhere. Okay?"

"I hope she's good looking," the stocky man said. "If I got to go all through that so your wife doesn't know where you are, I sure hope she's good looking, is all I can say."

4

"YOU REMEMBER Eddie Fingers," Dave said. "Eddie Coyle? Fellow that got his hand busted up after they put Billy Wallace away for a long time on a gun that he bought from somebody. Got himself in a whole mess of trouble up in New Hampshire trucking a little booze that didn't belong to him about this time last year."

"He the bank robber?" Waters asked. "The one from Natick?"

"That's his sidekick," Dave said, "Artie Van. Arthur Valantropo. Eddie doesn't rob banks. He's a thief. Doesn't go in for that kind of rough stuff, although I suppose he was down on his luck, he might take a crack at almost anything."

"I was thinking of another guy," Waters said. "Hangs around Artie Van too. Van went in on a carrying charge and this guy was up to see him all the time. Looked like he had smallpox or something."

"Doesn't mean anything to me," Dave said.

"Italian name," Waters said. "It'll come to me. All I can think of right now is Scanlon, and that sure isn't it."

"Yeah," Dave said, "well, I had this call from Coyle the other day, so I went out to see him."

"I thought we loaned you to Narcotics," Waters said.

"You did," Dave said. "I'll never be able to thank you enough. But this Coyle gets around, I thought maybe he had something to say about drugs."

"Shit," Waters said.

"I was terrible disappointed," Dave said. "I said so at the time."

"What'd he want?" Waters said.

"He's coming up for sentencing in New Hampshire after the first of the year," Dave said.

"He wants some references," Waters said.

"That was what he had in mind," Dave said. "What he said he had in mind, anyway."

"What's he got to trade?" Waters said.

"Black militants," Dave said. "Claims he knows about some group that's buying machineguns."

"Believe him?" Waters said.

"I think he was telling me the truth," Dave said. "I think what he was telling me was the truth, anyway. He said he didn't know much and he didn't, not about that, anyway."

"There probably isn't very much to know," Waters said. "I never seen such a bunch of pigeons on black militants since we started getting a wise guy or two every so often. The Panthers're the best thing ever happened to the Mafia, far as they're concerned. They'll trade you ten niggers for one wop any day of the week. I think it's beautiful."

"It has its points," Dave said. "I'd damned sight rather see the wise guys trading off Panthers'n see the wise guys trading with Panthers."

"There's talk they're doing that," Waters said.

"I don't think so," Dave said. "Not around here, anyway. I don't doubt they drink from the same water holes, but they're not working together. Not yet. The wise guys're bigots, you know."

"Scalisi," Waters said. "The guy that hangs around with Artie Van is Jimmy Scalisi. Somewhat of a hard guy, a bad bastard from the word go. Dolan and Morrissey from SP Concord were trying to get Artie Van turned around when he was up at the farm there, Billerica, and Artie's going around and around, and the next thing you know, Scalisi and some friend of his're up to see him. Artie didn't say boo after that. I take it that Scalisi's some kind of craftsman with a pistol."

"That's what made me wonder," Dave said. "I dunno whether Eddie Fingers is telling me all he knows about the militants or not. He knows I'm a cop, of course, and he knows I'm a federal cop, so he's got to figure I got a hard-on for Panthers. Not that he ever said Panthers. But Eddie's not stupid. He's got something in mind. What I wonder is whether all he's got in mind is a recommendation from the government when he comes up for sentencing. I think maybe not."

"Why?" Waters said.

"How the hell did Eddie Fingers find out some black man's buying machineguns?" Dave said. "Does he hang around with black guys? Not this trip. So who else is involved? Somebody who's selling machineguns. Now why would Eddie Fingers be hanging around a guy who's selling machineguns?"

"Eddie Fingers is looking to pick up some guns," Waters said.

"Exactly," Dave said. "Eddie doesn't like machineguns, but he's gotten in the gravy before, supplying guns. That's how he got his hand smashed up. I think maybe Eddie's doing business again. I think he's talking to me so if somebody sees him doing business, it'll be all right, he's undercover."

"It'd be worth something to catch the guy he's doing business with," Waters said. "He's at least arming the wise guys, and maybe the Panthers too. I'd like a look at him. Can we put a tail on Eddie Coyle?"

"Sure," Dave said, "and he'll spot it six minutes out of the box. Eddie's not the bravest guy in the world, but he's not dumb and he's gotten very careful. That isn't the way to do it."

"What is the way to do it?" Waters said.

"The first thing is to get me off this dope kick I'm on," Dave said. "Nobody ought to object very much. So far, what I turned up, a sophomore in Weston High could produce on a warm afternoon."

"I'll see what I can do," Waters said. "Suppose you get off. What're you going to do then?"

"Eddie Coyle is a creature of habit," Dave said. "I'll work from that angle."

5

SEVEN AND A half miles east of Palmer, Route 20 bends to the north at the top of a hill, then banks away toward the south, leaving a rest area in a grove of pine trees. Late in the evening, a bearded young man swung a gold Karmann Ghia coupe onto the gravel parking area, shut off the headlights, and settled down to wait while his breath condensed on the inside of the windshield and the frost descended on the metal.

In the dark, Jackie Brown brought his Roadrunner off the Massachusetts Turnpike at Charlton, sent it hard through the ramp curves, and then vigorously west on Route 20. He arrived at the rest area fifteen minutes or so after the bearded man in the Karmann Ghia. He parked and switched off the ignition, then waited five minutes. The right directional signal of the Karmann Ghia flashed once. Jackie Brown got out of his car.

There was a strong smell of plastic, oil, and paint inside the Ghia. Jackie Brown said: "It's a good thing you told me you got a new car. I wouldn't've figured you for this. What happened to the Three-ninety-six?"

"I got my fucking insurance bill," the bearded man said. "Then I went out for a ride and I had to fill the goddamned thing, and it cost me nine bucks worth of superpremium, and I said the hell with it. Goddamn car was eating me blind."

"Went like a bird with a flame up its ass, though," Jackie Brown said.

"I'm getting too fucking old for that," the bearded man said. "I bust my ass all day to take home a hundred and seventy bucks a week and I just can't swing the kind of money it costs. I'm thinking about getting married and settling down."

"You been taking almost that off me," Jackie Brown said.

"Shit," the bearded man said. "Last six months I got you for thirty-seven hundred dollars. I spent that easy. I got to stop hacking around, is all. I keep this up, I'm gonna be behind bars before I'm through."

"Okay," Jackie Brown said, "it's a bad night. You got the stuff, is all I want to know. I got the money."

"I got two dozen," the bearded man said. He wrenched his body around and lifted a shopping bag out of the luggage bin behind the seats. "Most of them're four-inchers."

"That's all right," Jackie Brown said. "I got the money right here. Four-eighty, right?"

"Right," the bearded man said. "How come it's all right, four-inchers? Six months ago you used to piss and moan something awful, I brought you anything but two-inchers. All of a sudden it doesn't matter any more. How come?"

"I got a better class of trade," Jackie Brown said.

"Who the fuck're you dealing with?" the bearded man said. "You hooked in with the goddamned Mafia or something?"

Jackie Brown smiled. "Let me lay it right on you," he said. "I don't honestly know any more. I got this black guy that comes around every so often, but he's kind of short on dough, and besides, what he wants, you can't give. I got to get that from somebody else. Then I got this fat guy, about, oh, thirty-six, thirty-seven, and I'll be goddamned if I know what he does. Looks like a mick, but I don't even know his name. He wants me to think it's Paul, but I'm not sure. That son of a bitch'll take every piece I can deliver. Never seen such a man for guns. Four-inchers, six-inchers, thirty-eights, mags, forty-ones, forty-fives, forty-fours, you name it. He'll take anything, cash on the fucking barrelhead. That motherfucker'll go through a dozen guns in a week, come up begging for more. Now, you was to ask me, I'd be inclined to think he was in somewhere with the Mob, but then, he isn't about to tell me, and I'm not about to ask. He pays in American money is all that interests me. Same with the black guy. I was in Nassau for the weekend and I had me the sweetest piece of caramel ass you ever dreamed of, and that fat bastard that'll take anything, he paid for it. I think it's great. He can work for the Salvation Army if he wants, I don't care. He just keeps bringing money, it's all right with me."

"You do all right off me," the bearded man said.

"I give you twenty dollars apiece for iron that costs you fucking nothing," Jackie Brown said. "You never got a bit of feedback from me. I don't hassle you about nothing. I know what you're dumping the money on, I know all right, but as long as you can function, it's okay with me. You get my ass in the gears, I'll turn up the flame under yours. You could do ten years for what you're doing all by yourself. What you're doing for me is a sideline, and I know it. But it's a damned good sideline for you, and don't you forget it. I got a phone too. I can call the cops in Springfield just as fast as you can call them in Boston."

"Fuck you," the bearded man said.

"I'll see you next week," Jackie Brown said. "I want at least two dozen. I'll have the money."

6

DILLON EXPLAINED that he was frightened. "Otherwise I would help you, see?" he said. He sat on the bench on the Common in the midst of the insistent November sunshine, hunched over to protect his stomach. "I mean, I understand, what it is you got in mind, that you're willing to protect me. But I want to tell you this: you can't do it, you can't possibly do it. Because nobody can do it, you know? Nobody. This is something which I got into all by myself, and I am not going to get out of it."

Foley said nothing.

There were seven derelicts working their usual station down at the subway entrance at the corner of Boylston and Tremont Streets. Six of them sat along the retaining wall and discussed events of importance. They wore overcoats and hats and worn-out heavy shoes in the sunshine, partly because they were generally cold and partly because they had memories enough to know that winter was coming again, so that they would need the warm clothing which they did not dare to leave in the empty buildings where they slept. The youngest of the derelicts accosted businessmen and women who had been shopping. He worked diligently to keep them in front of him, trying to block their progress so that they would listen to him. It is harder to refuse to give a man a quarter after you have listened to him for a while, and noticed him. Not impossible, but harder. The younger derelict was still agile enough to maneuver, and could raise the price of a bottle of Petri faster than the others. Dillon watched him while he talked.

"I tell you what it is," he said. "The principal thing which bothers me is the truck. Now I know that sounds kind of funny, because I suppose you would think that what would be worrying me would be the guys in the truck or some guy I don't even know that I see maybe watching me pretty close in the bar or something."

North on Tremont Street, just beyond the Information Stand and the Fountain and the Parkman Bandstand, a couple of Jesus screamers were working a moderate crowd of clerks and secretaries and sightseers. The woman was tall. She had a good loud voice and a bullhorn to help it along. The man was short and walked around distributing leaflets. The wind delivered enough of what she was saying to distract Dillon from watching the derelicts..

"Now there is a strange thing," he said. "When I came up here I more or less take the long way around, to see if anybody else is interested and who that might be, you know? So I walk along and then I cross the street and come on back down past the pair of them there, and the woman says: 'Unless you accept Jesus, who is Christ the Lord, you shall perish, perish in the everlasting flames.'

"Now who am I to think about a thing like that, can you tell me that?" Dillon said. "Couple weeks ago these two gentlemen from Detroit came in and had a couple of drinks, and then they sort of look around and the next thing I know they inform me that we are going partners. They give me some time to think about it, you know, and while I think I make a few phone calls. So that when the few minutes are up I had maybe six or seven friends of mine in there and I took the opportunity to go out in the back and get a piece of pipe that I keep around. I hit them a couple of good ones and we throw them out in the street in front of a cab.

"Then two nights ago I get five of these Micmacs come in, real Indians, for a change, and they have a little firewater and begin to break up some of the furniture. So me and a few friends hadda use the pipe on them.

"So this broad hollers at me there, just a few minutes ago, about the everlasting flames, and I consider myself a fairly intelligent guy and all that, pretty good judgment, I get drunk once in a while now and then, but I got this strong idea I would like to go up with that piece of pipe under my coat and say: Well, what do I do about those fellows from Detroit, you want to tell me that? The Indians too. Jesus going to punish me for that? And then whack her once or twice across the snout to bring her to her senses."

The young bum had cornered a middleaged, rather stout businessman right in the middle of the mall, with open space all around. "I want to tell you something," Dillon said. "That kid may be a down-and-outer there, but he has pretty good moves. I think he used to be a basketball player, maybe.

"Anyway," he said, "I still got a certain amount of my sanity left and I didn't have the pipe with me, so I don't say anything to her and I don't bop her a couple, like I would like to. You can't reason with these people, you know. They get that idea in their heads, all they can do is stand there and bellyache Gospel at you, enough to drive a man out of what little mind he's got left.

"I knew this guy, met him when I was at Lewisburg on that federal thing back there three, four years ago. Forget what he was in there for, B and E in a federal building, maybe, post office job. Anyway, not a bad guy. Big, used to box some. He comes from down around New Bedford there. So we strike up a friendship.

"I get out first," Dillon said. "I come back here. I let him know where I am. So when they parole him, he goes home to live with his wife and her mother but he knows where I am if he needs to get ahold of me. And it wasn't very long before he needed to. Because those two women went right to work driving him out of his mind. Dumb Portuguese types, you know, and what did they do when he was in jail but they decide they don't want to be Catholics any more, they're going to be, what is it, Jehovah's Witnesses. Beautiful. Guy comes home, knows the construction business pretty good, gets himself a job, every night he comes home, there's maybe a ballgame on or something, they want him to go out and stand on the sidewalk in front of the supermarket, peddling Jesus to every poor bastard that comes around to get a pound of fish.

"So he starts coming up here," Dillon said, "every chance he gets, just to have a little peace and quiet. And the next thing I notice, he's coming up this one time and he doesn't go back. So I say to him, what're you doing here. And he says: 'For Christ sake, you aren't going to start in on me, are you?'

"I had some room," Dillon said. "I was separated from my wife at the time and I had some room. I let him stay with me. He drinks a bottle of beer and he watches the ballgame while I'm working and during the day, well, I don't know what he does. The best he can, probably.

"Naturally, it's just a matter of time the parole officer makes a report and says he's missing visits, which is true, and that his family says he doesn't come home, which is true, and that he's consorting with a known criminal, which is me and is also true, and he quit a steady job, whereabouts unknown. So one night the marshals come by and it's back to the can, parole violation. Drinking, too. I forgot that. I tell you, them two women preached that poor bastard right back into the can. You can't reason with people like that, doesn't do any good at all to talk to them."

Dillon straightened up and immediately bent forward again. The middleaged man executed a quick fake and got away from the younger derelict.

"That's the thing that bothers you, you know? It's just, well, there's some things you can help and some kinds of things you can't do anything about, is all. Knowing the difference, as long as you can tell the difference, you're in pretty good shape. That was what kind of bothered me about that big broad with the bullhorn there, was that just for a minute or so it was like I didn't know the difference. You get so you're in that position, you're not going to be able to do very much about anything."

The customary blizzard of pigeons wheeled briefly across the walk and settled back around an old lady who fed them from a large, wrinkled, paper bag. "I heard a guy on television the other night," Dillon said. "He was talking about pigeons. Called them flying rats. I thought that was pretty good. He had something in mind, going to feed them the Pill or something, make them extinct. Trouble is, he was serious, you know? There was a guy that got shit on and probably got shit on again and then he got mad. Ruined his suit or something, going to spend the rest of his life getting even with the pigeons because they wrecked a hundred-dollar suit. Now there isn't any percentage in that. There must be ten million pigeons in Boston alone, laying eggs every day, which will generally produce more pigeons, and all of them dropping tons of shit, rain or shine. And this guy in New York is going to, well, there just aren't going to be any of them in this world any more.

"You see what I'm telling you," Dillon said, "you should understand. I, it isn't that I don't trust you or anything. The man says you're all right, that does it for me. I accept that. But what you got in mind, if I do that I'll just have to spend the rest of my life, you know? Being somewhere, hiding out. And you cannot hide out, is all, you just cannot hide out.

"That guy I was telling you about," Dillon said, "his wife was the Jehovah Witness? Well, it didn't do anything to what she liked to do, and from what he was telling me, she liked to do that pretty often. Like, say, a couple times a night. In Lewisburg he used to tell me he was saving it up, no hand-gallops for him, because when he got home he was going to have to account for every ounce he owned. First time he comes up here, all pissed off, I asked him, well, at least how was that part? And he says to me, he says: 'You know something? There's one thing she always hated, it's going down on me. And ever since I get home, I been making her do it to get the other, because at least she's quiet when I'm making her do that.' You see what I mean? Man gets desperate, he does a few things, he knows it won't work, pretty soon he quits, just packs it all in and goes away somewhere. Only way there is.

"See, I know that," Dillon said. "If it's going to happen then it is going to happen. I don't know, some buddy of mine, that I probably refused to serve some night, started putting it around I been going out to see people he thinks I shouldn't. Which is true enough, of course, or else would I be here? But he's probably doing it too. Everybody's looking out for a little connection, you don't shit in the well because maybe you want to drink out of it some day. Anyway, the word's around there's this grand jury coming up, and the next thing I hear is, well, you know what I hear.

"I have seen the truck," Dillon said. "That is what impresses me. You put two guys in that truck and they could get the Pope. The only time I see an engine like that was in a Cadillac. So you don't, you aren't going to run away because that thing is going to run right away with you. And the windshield, the damned thing looks like an old bread truck, a milk truck, maybe, and the windshield cranks, it's got a crank on the passenger side and you can open it right up and run a deer rifle out there. You're driving a car in front of that truck and they want you, well, good luck to you. I understand they even got a gyro on it, you know? Like a fucking airplane. So they can lock on. Now you're on the Mystic Bridge and that thing wheels up behind you and the windshield's opening up, and I ask you, what're you going to do now? You're going to make a good Act of Contrition, is what you're going to do, because you got a choice between the rifle and the water and it doesn't matter much.

"Sure I don't drive. I could afford a car, I wouldn't be taking twenty a week from you. Only time I'm on the bridge is coming home from the track on the bus. But you see what I'm getting at. These guys're serious. I know them very well. You know that. They got a truck for guys that drive cars, they got something else for guys that walk, like me.

"You see what I'm telling you," Dillon said in the sunshine under the trees and the sky and the pigeons, "you see what I'm getting at. Right now they want to scare me, and they did it. I'm scared. I stay scared and I don't do anything anybody else isn't doing, I don't go into that grand jury there, maybe, just maybe, being scared is going to be enough. Satisfy them. He was scared and he didn't spook. Maybe not, too. But I go in there, I help you, whatever it is I got now, I am not going to have any more. I can walk around, and I can still tell the difference.

"I had this letter the other day from that guy I was telling you about, and you know what he said? He said: 'I got seven months to go and then I'm free and clear. No parole officer, no nothing. What I'm trying to decide is whether I kill that woman or not. I think right now I won't.'

"You see what I mean," Dillon said, "you're never sure. You are never sure what a man is going to do. I think if I was I wouldn't care, they wouldn't need that truck. I would kill myself."

"Okay," Dave said, "okay. Look, did I ever tell you we could keep you neat and clean? I ever give you that line of horseshit?"

"No," Dillon said. "No, you always been on the level. I give you that."

"Okay," Dave said. "I understand the position you're in. You can't talk about the Polack, you can't talk about the Polack. It's all right."

"Thanks," Dillon said.

"Screw," Dave said. "We been friends for a long time. I never asked a friend yet to do something he really couldn't do, when I knew he couldn't do it. The whole town's buttoned up on this grand jury anyway. I never seen things so quiet."

"There isn't much going on," Dillon said.

"Jesus," Dave said, "I know it. They got me on this detail, you know? Drugs. I been out of town probably three weeks now, I come back, and nothing's happening. I didn't miss a thing. You guys must've taken up circle-jerks or something. They ought to run one of those grand juries every three weeks or so. It sure puts you guys in the closet for a while. I don't care if they never catch those guys. Crime rate's down sixty per cent just making the hard guys worry about it."

"Fuck you," Dillon said.

"Hey look," Dave said. "There isn't anything going on. You can talk all you want, but the grand jury's got you guys up so tight you're choking on it. By the end of the week, Artie Van's going to be shining shoes or selling papers or maybe pimping or something. You oughta get unemployment."

"Cut it out," Dillon said.

"All right," Dave said, "that was a cheap shot. I apologize. But there isn't anything going on."

"There's something going on," Dillon said.

"Bunch of the boys getting together to watch dirty movies?" Dave said.

"You want the truth?" Dillon said. "I don't know what it is. People're sort of avoiding me. But something's going on. Guys calling up asking for guys that aren't there. I don't know what it is, but they got something going."

"Here's twenty," Dave said. "Who's calling up?"

"Remember Eddie Fingers?" Dillon said.

"Vividly," Dave said. "Who's he looking for?"

"Jimmy Scalisi," Dillon said.

"Is that so," Dave said. "And does he find him?"

"I dunno," Dillon said. "I'm just a messenger boy."

"They give you numbers," Dave said.

"Telephone numbers," Dillon said. "I got a liquor license. I'm a law-abiding citizen."

"You work for a guy that's got a liquor license," Dave said. "Ever see him? You're a convicted felon."

"You know how it is," Dillon said. "I work for a guy with a liquor license. I forget sometimes."

"Want to forget this?" Dave said.

"I'd just as soon," Dillon said.

"Merry Christmas," Dave said.

SAMUEL T. PARTRIDGE, having heard his wife and children descend the stairs, their bathrobes swishing on the Oriental runner, the little girls discussing nursery school, his son murmuring about breakfast, showered lazily and shaved. He dressed himself and went downstairs for eggs and coffee.

In the family room beyond the kitchen he saw his children standing close together next to the Boston rocker. His wife sat in the Boston rocker. All of their faces were blank. Three men sat on the couch. They wore blue nylon windbreakers over their upper bodies, and nylon stockings pulled down over their faces. Each of them held a revolver in his hand.

"Daddy, Daddy," his son said.

"Mr. Partridge," the man nearest him said. His features were frighteningly distorted by the nylon. "You are the first vice president of the First Agricultural and Commercial Bank and Trust Company. We are going to the bank, you and I and my friend here. My other friend will stay here with your wife and children, to make sure nothing happens to them. Nothing will happen to them, and nothing will happen to you, if you do what I tell you. If you don't, at least one of you will be shot. Understand?"

Sam Partridge swallowed both his rage and the sudden gout of phlegm that rose into his throat. "I understand," he said.

"Get your coat," the first man said.

Sam Partridge kissed his wife on the forehead. He

kissed each of his children. He said: "Don't be afraid, everything will be all right. Do what Mummy tells you. It'll be all right." Tears ran down his wife's cheeks. "Now, now," he said. "They don't want to hurt us, it's money they want." She started in his arms.

"He's right," the first man said. "We don't get any kicks at all from hurting people. It's the money. Nobody does anything silly, nobody gets hurt. Let's go to the bank, Mr. Partridge."

In the driveway behind the house there was a nondescript blue Ford sedan. Two men sat in the front seat. Each of them wore a nylon stocking over his head, and a blue windbreaker. Sam Partridge got into the back seat. The men from the house sat on each side of him. The driver said: "You sleep late, Mr. Partridge. We been waiting a long time."

"Sorry to inconvenience you," Sam Partridge said.

The man who talked in the house took charge of the conversation. "I know how you feel," he said. "I understand you're a brave man. Don't try to prove it. The man you're talking to has killed at least two people that I know about. I don't say what I've done. Just keep calm and be sensible. It isn't your money. It's all insured. We want the money. We don't want to hurt anybody. We will, but we don't want to. Are you going to be reasonable?"

Sam Partridge said nothing.

"I am going to gamble that you're going to be reasonable," the spokesman said. He took a blue silk kerchief from his jacket pocket and handed it to Sam Partridge. "I want you to fold this and put it over your eyes for a blindfold. I'll tie it for you. Then sit down on the floor of the car here."

The Ford began to move as Sam Partridge squirmed down between the seats. "Don't try to see anything," the spokesman said. "We have to take these stockings off until we get to the bank. When we get there, you just be patient until we get dressed up again. We'll go in the back door, the way you always do. You and I will stay together. Don't be concerned about my friends. Just tell your people not to unlock the front door and not to pull the curtains. We will wait until the time lock opens. My friends will take care of the vault. We will come back to this car when we've finished. You will explain to your people that they are not to call the police. You will tell them why they are not going to call the police. I know it's uncomfortable, but you will ride back to your house the same way you are now. We will get my friend at your house. When we get a safe distance away, we will let you go. Right now we don't plan to hit you on the head, but we will if you make us. Otherwise we don't plan to hurt you or anybody else, unless somebody fucks up. What you said was right: we want the money. Understood?"

Sam Partridge said nothing.

"You make life hard for me," the man said. "Since I have the pistol, that is not a good idea. Do you understand?"

"I understand," Sam Partridge said.

In the bank, Mrs. Greenan sobbed quietly as Sam Partridge explained the situation.

"Tell them about the alarm," the spokesman said.

"In a few minutes," Sam said, "the time lock on the vault will open. These men will take what they came for. I will then leave with them. We will return to my house. There is another man at my house, with my family. We will pick him up and leave. This man has told me that my family won't be hurt and that I will not be hurt if no one interferes with them. They will release me when they are satisfied that they have gotten away. I have no choice but to believe that they will do what they say. So I ask you, all of you, not to set off the alarms."

"Tell them to sit down on the floor," the spokesman said.

"Please sit down on the floor," Sam said. Mrs. Greenan and the others sat awkwardly.

"Go over to the vault," the spokesman said.

Next to the door to the vault, Sam Partridge had his field of vision contracted to include only two objects. There was a small clock set into the steel door of the vault. It stood at forty-five minutes past eight. There was no second hand. The minute hand did not appear to be moving. Eighteen inches away from the clock, down two feet from its eye-level location, there was the black-gloved hand of the spokesman. It held, very steadily, a heavy revolver. Sam saw that there was some kind of a rib on the barrel, and that the handle was molded out to cover the top of the hand that held it. He saw touches of gold inside the black metal of the cylinders. The hammer of the revolver was drawn back to full cock. The minute hand did not seem to have moved.

"What time does it open?" the spokesman said quietly.

"Eight-forty-eight," Sam said absently.

In July they had taken the children to New Hampshire and rented a cottage on a palette-shaped pond north of Centerville. They had rented a boat one morning, an aluminum rowboat, with a small motor, and he had taken the children fishing while his wife slept. Around eleven they had come in because his son wanted to go to the bathroom. They beached the rowboat and the children ran up the gravel slope to the tall grass, and through the tall grass in the sunshine to the cabin. Sam had removed a string of four pickerel from the boat and placed it on the gravel. He had bent back to lift out the rods and the tackle box and the thermos of milk and the sweaters. He straightened up with the articles and turned toward where he had placed the fish.

On the loose gravel of the shore, perhaps a foot from the stringer of fish, a thick brown timber rattler was coiled. Its head was perhaps a foot off the ground. The rattles of its tail lay drooped against one of its fat coils. It had been swimming; its smooth, textured body was wet, and it glistened in the sun. The patterns of brown and black repeated themselves regularly along the skin. The eyes of the snake were glossy and dark. Its delicate black tongue flickered out, without a discernible opening of its jaws. The skin beneath the jaws was creamy. The sun had fallen comfortably warm upon the thick snake and upon Sam, who was repeatedly chilled, and he and the snake had remained motionless, except for the snake's black, delicate tongue which flickered in and out from time to time, for several lifetimes. Sam had begun to feel faint. The position in which he had frozen, almost erect, with the children's articles and the tackle in his hands, made his muscles ache. The snake appeared relaxed. It made no sound. Sam could think of nothing but his uncertainty; he did not know whether rattlers struck without rattling. Again and again he reminded himself that it made no difference, that the snake could easily satisfy any such ritual quickly enough to hit him before he could get away. Again and again the question nagged at him. "Now look," he had said at last to the snake, "you can have the goddamned fish. You hear me? You can have them."

The snake had remained in the same position for a time. Then its coils had begun to straighten. Sam had decided to try to jump if it came toward him. He knew that it could swim faster than he in the water, and he had no weapon. The snake completely controlled the situation. The snake turned slowly on the gravel, its weight rubbing the pebbles against each other. It proceeded up the slope, diagonally away from the cabin. In a while it was gone, and Sam, his body aching, rested the articles on the seats of the boat, and began to tremble.

The spokesman said: "What time does it say now?"

Sam swung his eyes back from the black revolver to the clock. "It doesn't seem to move," he said. "Eight forty-seven, I think. It really isn't much good for telling time. All it does is show the mechanism is working, really."

When he had told his wife about the snake, she had wanted to leave at once and give up the four days remaining on the cabin rental. And he had said: "We've been here what, nine days? That snake's been here all his life, and he's big enough so it's been a long time. There's probably a snake somewhere else in New England, too. The children haven't gotten bitten so far. There's no reason to think he's going to get more aggressive between now and Saturday. We can't spend our lives in Ireland just because the kids might get bitten by a snake some time." They had stayed. But they had noticed themselves picking their way through the long grass, and watching carefully where they stepped on the gravel, and when they were in the water, Sam was constantly watching for the small head and the thick shiny coils in the blue pond.

"Do you want to try it now?" the spokesman said. "Or does it set off the alarm if you try it before the set time?"

"No," Sam said. "It just doesn't open. But there's a click when it hits the set time. There isn't any use in trying it until you hear that click."

There was a dry snap inside the door of the safe. "There it is," Sam said. He began to turn the wheel.

The spokesman said: "When you get it open, move over toward the desks there, so I can watch you and the rest of them at the same time."

Sam stood near his own desk, staring at the pictures of his family, pictures that he had taken. There was a Zenith desk set with two pens and an AM-FM radio in the front center area; his wife had given it to him for company when he had to work late. Yesterday's *Wall Street Journal* lay folded on the near corner of the desk. Mrs. Greenan collected the mail each morning and brought him the *Journal* before sorting the rest of it. Her routine had been interrupted. She would be helpless all day. In the morning, regular customers would be calling to inquire about their deposits and withdrawals, because the tickets and checks would not arrive when expected. No, that was not correct: there would be something in the papers about this, something on television.

The other two men converged from the positions

they had taken up in the bank. Each of them produced a bright green plastic bag from under his coat, and shook it out. They went into the vault. They did not speak. The black revolver remained steady.

The other two men emerged from the vault. They placed the green plastic bags on the floor. One of them produced another bag and shook it out. He went back into the vault. The second man drew his gun and nodded.

The spokesman said: "When he comes out, you remind your people about the alarm. Then tell them there is going to be some shooting, but no one's going to get hurt. I'm going to have to take out those cameras you got there."

"Why do you bother?" Sam said. "Those are for people who cash bad checks that you ordinarily don't notice in the course of business. Everybody in here's been staring at you guys for the past ten minutes. They can't identify you. Why take the chance? There's a drugstore next door and he's open by now. If you think this place is soundproof, it isn't. You start shooting and you'll bring somebody for sure."

"Helpful, aren't you?" the spokesman said.

"I don't want to get hurt and I don't want anybody else to get hurt," Sam said. "You said you'd use that thing. I believe you. Those cameras haven't seen anything I haven't seen: just a bunch of frightened people and three men with stockings over their faces. You got to kill all of us, too."

"All right," the spokesman said. The third man came out of the vault, the third bag partly full. "Tell them this: my friends're going to go out and get in the car. Then we're going out and get in the car and go back to your house. Your people're to open the bank and say absolutely nothing to nobody for at least an hour. If they do that, maybe you won't get killed."

"Will you listen to me, please?" Sam said. "We're going to leave now. As soon as the door shuts in the back, get up and take your usual places. Open the doors and pull the curtains. Start to do business as usual, as best you can. It's very important that these men have at least an hour to get away. I know it'll be difficult for you. Do the best you can, and if anyone comes in wanting a large amount of cash, you'll have to tell them there's something wrong with the vault and we've called a repairman to open it."

To the spokesman, he said: "Will you have one of your friends there close the vault?"

The spokesman pointed toward the vault door. The second man swung it shut. The spokesman nodded and the two men picked up the plastic bags and disappeared into the corridor leading to the back door.

"Please remember what I've said," Sam said. "Everything depends on you to see that no one gets hurt. Please do your very best."

In the car there was no sign of the plastic bags. Then Sam noticed that one of the men was missing. He sat in the back seat with the spokesman. The driver started the engine.

"Now, Mr. Partridge," the spokesman said, "I'm going to ask you to put this blindfold on again and get down on the floor of the car. Me and my friend in the front're going to take off the stockings. When we get to your house I will help you out of the car. You'll take the blindfold off so nobody gets frightened. We'll pick up my other friend and come back out to the car. You'll put the blindfold on again, and everything goes all right, in a little while you'll be safe and sound. Understand?"

In the family room his wife and children seemed to occupy the same places they had had when he first came downstairs. His wife sat in the rocker and the children stood close together next to her. He knew without being told that they had not spoken since he left. The fourth man rose from the couch as they entered.

Sam said: "I've got to go away with these men for a little while now, and then everything'll be all right, okay?" The children did not answer. To his wife, he said: "You better call the school and tell them we've all got the bug and the children'll be absent."

"Don't say anything else," the spokesman said.

"I'm just trying to do what you told me," Sam said. "The school calls if you don't."

"Fine," the spokesman said. "Just make sure it isn't the State Police or something. Now, let's go."

Outside, Sam was blindfolded again. His eyes hurt from the sudden change from sunlight to darkness. He was led to the car. He was pushed down on the floor. He heard the car go into gear, the transmission under his head clinking as the car backed up. He felt it lurch forward. He was able to tell as it turned out of the driveway and turned left. When it came to a stop and turned right, he knew it was on Route 47. The car proceeded for a long time without stopping. Sam searched his memory for the number of stop lights or signs that they would have passed. He could not remember. He was unable to say any longer where they were. There was no conversation in the car. Once he heard a match being struck, and soon after smelled a cigarette burning. He thought: We must be getting somewhere. It must be almost over.

There was a crunching sound under the car and it slowed down quickly. The spokesman said: "I'm going to open the door now. Put your hands on the seat and get yourself sitting up. I'll take your arm and get you out of the car. We're at the edge of a field. When you get out, I'll point you and you start walking. You'll hear me get back in the car. The window will be down. I'll be pointing the gun at you every minute. You just start walking and you walk as far as you can. Sometime while you're walking, you'll hear the car move off the shoulder here. I promise you, we'll stay parked on the pavement for a while. You won't be able to tell by listening whether we're still here or not. Count to one hundred. Then take your mask off and hope to God we're gone."

Sam was cramped and stiff from lying on the floor. He stood unsteadily on the shoulder of the road. The spokesman took his arm and led him into the field. He could tell he was standing in wet, long grass. "Start walking, Mr. Partridge," the spokesman said. "And thanks for your cooperation."

Sam heard the car move off the gravel. He shuffled along in the darkness, the unevenness of the field frightening him. He was afraid of stepping into a hole. He was afraid of stepping on a snake. He got up to thirty-four and lost count. He counted again to fifty. He was unable to breathe. No longer, he thought, no longer. I can't wait any longer. He removed the blindfold, expecting to be shot. He was alone in a broad, level pasture bordered by oaks and maples that had lost their leaves and stood black in the warm November morning. For a moment he stood blinking, then turned and looked at the empty road scarcely twenty yards away. He began to run, stiffly, toward the road.

8

AT FIVE minutes of six, Dave Foley escaped from the traffic on Route 128 and parked the Charger at the Red Coach Grille in Braintree. He went into the bar and took a table in the rear corner that allowed him to watch the door and the television set above the bar. He ordered a vodka martini on the rocks with a twist. After a white man strenuously stated the headlines, the evening news report began. As the waitress arrived with Foley's drink, a black man with heavy jowls and an accent that made *er* sounds into *or* sounds delivered the first story.

"Four gunmen, masked with nylon stockings, made off with an estimated ninety-seven thousand dollars from the First Agricultural and Commercial Bank and Trust Company in Hopedale this morning," he said. "The bandits invaded the Dover home of bank official Samuel Partridge shortly before dawn. Leaving one to hold the family hostage, they forced Partridge to accompany them to the bank. Employees were held at gunpoint while the robbers looted the vault of most of the bank's currency, leaving only coins and a few small bills behind. Partridge was then driven back to his home, where the robbers picked up the guard they had left. After being blindfolded, Partridge was turned loose on Route 116 in Uxbridge, near the Rhode Island line. A blue Ford, apparently the getaway car, was found two miles away. The FBI and the State Police have entered the case. Partridge told me this afternoon. . . ."

A bulky black man wearing a double-breasted blue silk suit came into the bar and paused for an instant. Foley stood up and waved him over.

"Deetzer," Foley said, "how goes the battle for equal rights?"

"We're definitely losing," the black man said. "This morning I told her I wouldn't be home for dinner, and now I got to empty the garbage for three months, and take the kids to the zoo Saturday."

"What do you hear, Deetzer old man," Foley said.

"I hear they serve a drink here now and then," the black man said. "Can I get one of those?"

Foley signaled the waitress and pointed to his glass. Then he raised two fingers.

"Are we eating here, Foles?" the black man said.

"Might as well," Foley said. "I could use a steak."

"Is uncle paying?" the black man said.

"I wouldn't be surprised," Foley said.

"I'm beginning to remember hearing some things now," the black man said. "What shall we talk about?"

"I been thinking about going into the holdup business," Foley said. "What I want to do is get up an integrated gang. We'd be invincible, Deetzer. Four bastards no smarter'n you and me got ninety-seven K out of some little bank in the woods this morning, no muss, no fuss, no bother. And here we are, deserving young men, family types, hacking along on a fucking salary."

"I heard on the radio a hundred and five thousand," the black man said.

"Well there you are, Deetzer," Foley said. "A day's work and all they got to worry about now is the Effa-Bee-Eye. You'll be trotting the garbage from now until Easter, they'll be getting a tan on the beach at

Antigua, and I'll be beating the bushes with snow to my jock until Washington's Birthday, tracking down housewives who pay ten bucks for six ounces of Lipton Tea and two ounces of bad grass."

"I was thinking about joining a commune," the black man said. "I heard about this place up near Lowell, everybody welcome, you take off your clothes and screw all day and drink boysenberry wine all night. Trouble is, I hear all they get to eat is turnips."

"You're too old for a commune," Foley said. "They wouldn't take you. You couldn't get it up enough to meet the specs. What you need is some government-funded job with a secretary that comes in every afternoon, strips down to the garter belt, and gets it up for you."

"I applied for that job," the black man said. "I know just the one you mean. Pays thirty grand a year and you get a Cadillac and a white man to drive it. They told me it was filled. Some kid from Harvard Law School, got hair down to his navel and a beard and wears boots. They said I wasn't qualified to lead the people to the promised land, what they needed was a nice Jewish boy that didn't wash."

"I thought they had their rights," Foley said.

"So did I," the black man said. "It's the jobs they want now."

"The brothers will be very uptight when they hear this," Foley said. "Should I call Military Intelligence and tell them to load and holster their movie cameras for an imminent demonstration?"

"Probably not," the black man said. "The way to handle it is to pass the word to some crabby dumb mick of a DA, and he'll bugger it up fast enough."

"Would a City Councilman do?" Foley said.

"Even better," the black man said. "Better still, a City Councilwoman. They're the best. You know where they stand."

"How are the brothers, anyway?" Foley said.

"Ah, Deetzer, Deetzer, you never learn," the black man said. "Whenever the white man calls, it's because he's got a hard-on for the Panthers again. Is it the Panthers this time, Foles?"

"I dunno," Foley said. "I dunno who it is. I don't even know if it is, to tell you the truth. I'd be very surprised to find out it was Panthers. From what I read in the papers, they spend most of their time in court for shooting each other."

"Not all of them," the black man said. "The rank and file run a catering business."

"Any of them looking out to buy some machineguns?" Foley asked.

"I suppose so," the black man said. "They run around all the time saying: 'Off the pigs.' I was doing that, I'd want some machineguns around for when the pigs get mad."

"Do you know of anybody looking to buy machineguns?" Foley said.

"Come on, Dave," the black man said, "you know me: white man's nigger. I don't know any more about the Panthers'n you do. Or any other brothers. Am I the best you can do? Haven't you guys got somebody in there that can tip you? I mean, you asking me, you need help bad. You want to know what I hear on the street, I can tell you. But I'm on the government tit, too. Different government and all, but still on the government tit. The brothers don't talk to me. Oh, they talk to me, but they don't talk serious. If they were buying cannons, they wouldn't tell me about it."

"Deetzer," Dave said, "I need a favor. I want you to go out and see what you can hear. I got a line that the brothers're mobbing up, getting guns from somebody that's in with the wise guys. The idea kind of bothers me."

"Jesus," the black man said, "competition I heard of. There's always some lunatic looking around to take the numbers action. But a treaty? News to me."

"News to me, too," Foley said. "See what you can find out, huh Deets?"

9

JACKIE BROWN found the tan Microbus on the upper level of the Undercommon Garage, near the stairs to the kiosk at Beacon and Charles Streets. The interior of the vehicle was dark. There were flowered curtains covering all of the windows behind the front seat. He rapped on the driver's window.

There appeared at the window a puffy face surrounded by straggly blond hair, collar length. The face contained two suspicious eyes. Jackie Brown stared back at it. In a while, a hand came up and opened the vent window. The face also had a voice. "Whaddaya want?" it said.

"What do *you* want?" Jackie Brown said. "A man told me you wanted something."

"That's not good enough," the voice said.

"Fuck you," Jackie Brown said. He turned around and began walking.

The left rear window swung open. Another voice, lighter, said: "Are you selling something?"

"That depends," Jackie Brown said.

"Wait a minute," the lighter voice said.

Jackie Brown turned around. He did not walk back. He was about twelve feet from the bus. He waited.

The puffy face reappeared at the driver's window. The vent window opened again. The voice said: "Are you a cop?"

Jackie Brown said: "Yes."

The voice said: "Don't hassle me, man. Are you the guy we're looking for?"

"That depends," Jackie Brown said. "That depends on what you're looking to do."

"Wait a minute," the voice said. The face withdrew. Then it reappeared. "Come to the back door."

At the back door Jackie Brown found a young girl inviting him in. She looked like Mia Farrow. He stared at her. "Who're you?"

"Come inside," she said.

Inside the bus there was a small sink and a double bed. There was a portable radio, AM-FM-Police Band. On the bed there was a forty-five automatic. A great many paperback books lay on the floor. There was a sharp-smelling smoke.

"Look," Jackie Brown said, "I came here to do business. You people want to fuck and blow a little pot, what the hell did you bring me for? I understood there was going to be somebody here that wanted to do business."

The puffy face came in from the front. "This is Andrea," the voice said. "I'm Pete."

"I'm Jackie," Jackie Brown said. "What the hell is Andrea doing here?"

"This is Andrea's," the voice said, the hands indicating the bus. "Andrea's got the money. Andrea wanted to see you."

"I wanted to see you," Andrea said.

"I'm sorry," Jackie Brown said, "I must have the wrong number. I thought I was supposed to see somebody that wanted to buy something."

"You were expecting a black," Andrea said.

"Yeah," Jackie Brown said.

"That was Milt," she said. "He's with us. Milt is with us. He was talking about us. We were the people who wanted to see you."

"What about?" Jackie Brown said.

"We understood you could get us some machineguns," Andrea said in a soft voice.

"Look," Jackie Brown said, "you want to burn your fucking bra, all right. What the fuck do you want with a machinegun?"

"I want to hold up a fucking bank," she said.

"I can get you five machineguns by Friday," Jackie Brown said. "M-sixteen rifles. Three hundred and fifty dollars apiece. You want ammo, it's extra."

"How much extra?" Andrea said.

"Two hundred and fifty dollars for five hundred rounds," Jackie Brown said.

"That's two thousand dollars," Andrea said.

"More or less," Jackie Brown said.

"Be here Friday night with the stuff," she said.

"Half now," Jackie Brown said. "Machineguns're hot items. A grand in advance."

"Give him a thousand dollars, Pete," Andrea said.

Jackie Brown accepted a packet of money. It consisted of twenty fifties.

"Friday night at eight-thirty," she said.

"Friday afternoon at three-thirty," Jackie Brown said, "you call this number and ask for Esther. Someone will tell you that Esther stepped out, and ask you for a number. Stay in the pay phone after you give the number. Hold the handset up to your ear and pretend to be talking. But hold the cradle down. The phone will ring in three minutes. You'll get directions to a place that you can reach in forty minutes from downtown Boston. Forty-five minutes after you get those directions, the machineguns will be gone from that place, and you'll lose your deposit."

"I don't like that," Pete said.

"I don't give a good fuck what you like," Jackie Brown said. "I got two problems selling machineguns to people like you. The first is selling machineguns. That's life in this State. The second is selling to people like you. You aren't honest. You know where I'm going to be, and what time, I'm liable not to get the rest of my money. I'm liable to lose my machineguns. Another thing: you have the rest of the money with you. You show up with no money, no guns. And *you* show up. Keep this in mind. I got more than five machineguns. The rest'll be pointed at you."

"Bastard," Andrea said.

"Life's hard," Jackie Brown said, "life's very hard. Good night."

10

THE STOCKY MAN seemed pressed for time, and had no patience for conversation. He said to Jackie Brown: "You owe me ten more guns. I need them fast. When am I going to get them?"

Jackie Brown shrugged slightly. "Jesus, I don't know. I got you the first batch when I said, and I was a week ahead on the dozen. I'm doing the best I can, you know. These things sometimes take time."

"Time is what I haven't got," the stocky man said. "I told you the kind of people I deal with. I'm getting pressure. Tomorrow night I'm supposed to see the man. I need the guns."

"I can't get them for you by tomorrow night," Jackie Brown said. "I can't possibly get them to you before the weekend. You got to understand, the factory just makes one thing at a time. When you get a mixed batch, it's because you're getting some of the last batch and some of the batch they're making now. I don't even know what they're turning out. Maybe the new stainless stuff. I just don't know. It'll take me a couple days to find out what's available."

"I don't care whether it's the stainless or not," the stocky man said. "I got to have the stuff tomorrow night. I got a long ride and I got to have the stuff with me when I make it."

"No day," Jackie Brown said. "No day, no way. No can do. I told you: I get quality stuff. It takes some time. It isn't like buying a fucking loaf of bread. I got a thing set up that works pretty good, dependable stuff that won't get anybody in trouble. I'm not going to screw it up just because your people've got hot pants. I got to think of the future. You'll have to tell them: Wait. The stuff'll come. What's the big emergency, anyway?"

"One of the first things I learn is not to ask a man why he's in a hurry," the stocky man said. "The man says he's in a hurry and I already told him he could depend on me, because you told me I could depend on you. Now things're working out different, and one of us is going to have a big fat problem. Now let me tell you something, kid," the stocky man said, "that's another thing I learn. When one of us're going to have a problem, you're going to be the one, I got anything to say about it."

"Now look," Jackie Brown said.

"Now look, nothing," the stocky man said, "I'm getting old. I spent my whole life sitting around in one crummy joint after another with a bunch of punks like you, drinking coffee, eating hash, and watching other people take off for Florida while I got to sweat how the hell I'm going to pay the plumber next week. I've done time and I stood up, but I can't take no more chances. You can give me a whole ration of shit and this and that, and blah, blah, blah. But you, you're still a kid and you're going out and coming around and saying: 'Well, I'm a man, you can take what I say and it'll happen. I go through.' Well, you're learning something too, kid, and I advise you, you better learn it now, because when you say that, when you get me out there all alone on what you say, well, you better be there in back of me. Because once you say it's going to happen, *it's going to fucking happen*, and if it doesn't you got your

cock caught in the zipper but good. Now I don't want
no talk and shit from you. I want ten guns from you
and I got the money to pay for them, and I want them
tomorrow afternoon at the place where we were before,
and I'm going to be there and you're going to be there
with those goddamned guns. Because if you're not, I'm
going to come looking for you, and I'll find you, too, because I'm not going to be the only one that's looking
and we know how to find people."

"I got to go to Rhode Island tonight," Jackie Brown
said. "I'll be back late. I got to see some people late tomorrow afternoon. Can I meet you early some place tomorrow? So I can get free by, say, three o'clock?
Because you're coming up faster'n we said, you know,
and I already told you, I got other people I see too."

"Tomorrow afternoon's okay," the stocky man said.
"I'll see you tomorrow afternoon at the same place we
were before. You still got that Plymouth?"

"Yeah," Jackie Brown said, "but that's no good for
me. Too far from here. I got to be around here by four.
I can't make it. I don't want, I can't afford to take no
chances. Got to be somewhere around here."

"You know where the Fresh Pond Shopping Center
is?" the stocky man said. "Cambridge?"

"Yeah," Jackie Brown said.

"There's a grocery store there," the stocky man said,
"and a five-and-ten. I'll be in one of the stores there tomorrow at three o'clock. You drive in and park. I'll see
you. If it's all right, if I think it's all right, I'll come out
and we can get this thing over with. Don't wait no
more'n ten minutes. If I don't come out, something isn't
right. Leave and go to where I got that number for you,
and I'll call you there and we'll set something else up."

"You got a tail?" Jackie Brown said.

"Next month I'm getting sentenced up in New Hampshire," the stocky man said. "I can't afford no bust right now, for anything. I got to be careful."

"Yeah," Jackie Brown said, "but if it don't come off over there, I'm not going back to where you got me before. I can't do that. It'll have to be tomorrow night if it burns tomorrow afternoon. You call and say what time, and leave me a number or something, and I'll be where you say."

"All right," the stocky man said. "I'll look for you tomorrow."

"Have the money," Jackie Brown said. "Six bucks. Have it there. I work this fast, I'm going to need money fast."

"No sweat," the stocky man said. "I'll have the money."

11

Foley explained the delay. "I got your call from the office," he said. "I was out in the woods there. I came as fast as I could. What's on your mind?"

Along the Lafayette Mall, the streetlights disposed of the gloom of the autumn early evening. Near the first subway kiosk the Hare Krishnas sang and danced, wearing saffron robes and tattered gray sweaters and sneakers with no socks.

"I didn't mind," Dillon said. "I'm not in any hurry myself, but I thought, I thought maybe this was something you might be in a hurry about. I been sitting here watching them goddamned fools with their pigtails and paint on their faces, jumping around, and they got this kid with them, looks just like a little German, or a Swede, maybe, and there's his Mummy and Daddy jumping around like a couple of maniacs, playing Indian. That poor little kid. When he grows up, what the hell is he going to do? I was him, I think I'd shoot somebody. I'd start with Mummy and Daddy, for openers."

"Hey look," Foley said, "they don't hurt nobody."

"I know that," Dillon said. "I know that all right, but I see them going up to people and they're really serious, you know? They mean it. They think we all oughta take off our pants and put on them nightgowns and go humping around beating on a goddamned drum. They also think we're going to do it. Now that's crazy, isn't it? Sure it's crazy, but then I think: I was here when they come up and I see they got this brand-new Olds, which I assume they get with the money they bum off the sensible people, and now I'm wondering, who is it that's crazy? Is it them getting goose pimples jumping around in front of God and all the people, or is it me? I don't have a new Olds, all I got is a card for next week on which I was stupid enough to take the Pats again. I never learn."

"What'd you want to see me about?" Foley said.

"Hey," Dillon said, "remember last time I saw you, you're giving me a little leg about there's nothing going on? And I said no, there's something but I don't know what it is? Well, I was right, wasn't I?"

"Depends on what you mean," Foley said. "There's some things going on, but I don't see any of the boys making a buck out of it."

"Well," Dillon said, "now you never know. But look, you asked me, what's going on, and I told you, people making telephone calls. I'm always getting calls for people that aren't there, and pretty soon the guy that isn't there shows up, or maybe I get another telephone call and it's from him, and he wants to know, is anybody calling for me? Now there isn't that many guys that've got something going and they don't want their wife to find out. Remember that?"

"Yeah," Foley said. "You said Eddie Fingers was having something to do with Scalisi."

"I mentioned Eddie Fingers," Dillon said, "and I mentioned Scalisi too. I don't remember saying they had something working. They were just two of the guys I was talking about, that had a lot of time to spend on the telephone. That fucking Coyle, I don't see how he can walk, he must have so many dimes in his pockets. You throw him in the water, he'd sink like a fucking stone, he's so heavy."

"Okay," Foley said, "Eddie's making a lot of calls."

"I ain't seen Scalisi around in a while," Dillon said.

"I heard that," Foley said. "Nobody has. I heard he was down in Florida getting some sun."

"I heard he wasn't," Dillon said. "I heard he made a lot of money recently."

"That so," Foley said. "All by himself?"

"Sure," Dillon said. "You know Jimmy, everybody likes him. I imagine some friend of his give him a good tip on a horse or something, you know?"

"It's good to have friends," Foley said.

"Certainly is," Dillon said. "I had a call from Scalisi there yesterday night, and the fellow he wanted wasn't around, so I say, sure, I'll have him call you soon as he gets in. You got a number? And he says: 'I'm not going to be here very long. I tell you, it's kind of important. Why don't you tell him soon as you see him, it's important and I want to talk with him, and that'll probably do it.'"

"Uh huh," Foley said.

"So this afternoon," Dillon said, "I'm in there as usual and listening to the feature at the Rock and getting my brains whipped out as usual, and probably I sold four dollars' worth of beer all day, nobody drinks a straight shot any more, and who comes in but the fellow that Jimmy Scal calls about yesterday. So I finish out of the money as usual, old Babe never did me no good, and then I go up to him and he's got this kind of a tense expression on his face, like he thinks maybe he's got his tit caught in the wringer, and I say to him, you know, what'll you have and all, and he orders a shot and a beer, bless my soul. So I bring it up, and I'm giving him a little gas, you know, one thing and another, and then I remember, because I got so many people calling in, I remember that this guy is one of the guys they been calling in for. So I say to him: 'Hey, Jimmy Scal get in touch with you?'

"Well," Dillon said, "he gets this look on his face and he says: 'No, I didn't know he was looking for me.' And from the way he looks I think it's probably just as well he didn't, he looked like somebody knocked the whey out of him.

"So I say: 'Yeah, he called last night, looking for you. Said it was important. He didn't get in touch with you, huh?' See, I'm giving it to him a little bit.

" 'No,' he says, 'no, I told you he didn't. He leave a number?'

"So I'm standing there, still playing Mickey the Dunce, all these guys running around like mad all over the countryside, keeping in touch by calling me up, I practically haven't got time to pour the booze, I'm so busy answering the fucking phone, but nobody trusts me all the same, see, I'm just the switchboard operator. So I'm entitled to some of my own. And I say: 'Jesus, no. I asked him for one and he says to me, he says he's leaving and just to tell you it's important, he wants to talk with you.'

"That party sits there," Dillon said, "and all of a sudden, whomp, he's got that shot down and the beer running right after it, and I actually think he's getting white. 'Do it again, quick,' he says, 'gimme another one.' So I pour him another one. He gets back on that one just as fast, throws some money onna bar and backs off the stool, you know, like he hadda go to the john and quick, too. 'I'm leaving,' he says. 'Around an hour or so, I'll call back in, see if anybody called, and if they did, you tell me, and when they do, well, say I'm going to the place and I'll be there as soon as I see a fellow. Okay?'

"Okay with me, is what I say," Dillon says, "and he goes out. Now what do you make of that?"

"Who was this party?" Foley said.

"That's what interested me," Dillon said. "It was Eddie Coyle. Funny, huh?"

12

"THE DUCK sent me," Jackie Brown said to the battered green door on the third floor landing of the tenement house. There was a strong smell of vegetables around him.

The door opened slowly, without any sound. Light trickled out around the edge and Jackie Brown's eyes refocused again in the thick air. He could see the side of a man's head, one eye and an ear and part of the nose. At waist level he saw two hands gripping the stump of a double-barreled shotgun that was less than a foot long. "What does the Duck want?" the man said. He hadn't shaved for a few days.

"The Duck wants me to help him sometimes," Jackie Brown said, "and I did. Now he wants you to help me, on account of it."

"What kind of help exactly?" the stubbled man said.

"Suppose I was to say I wanted ten pieces and had cash to pay for them right now?" Jackie Brown said. "Would that help you out?"

The door opened fully and the stubbled man backed away from it, still holding the shotgun at waist level. "Come in," he said. "I assume you know what I can do with this thing if I was to decide I didn't like what you were saying. Come in and tell me what you got in mind."

Jackie Brown entered the apartment. It was furnished with white shag wall-to-wall carpeting, heavy orange drapes, and black chairs. There was a large, low table made of glass and chromium before a black

leather couch. There were gold and orange pillows on
the couch. A girl with long, blonde hair, wearing a
white cashmere jumpsuit, unzipped deeply in the front
with no bra under it, sat curled up on the couch. From
hidden speakers, Jackie Brown heard Mick Jagger and
the Rolling Stones singing. Illuminated by a globular
white lamp hanging from a silver arm was a poster that
said in orange on white: "Altamont. This Is The Next
Time."

"Pretty nice," Jackie Brown said.

The stubbled man said: "Leave us alone, Grace."

The girl arose and left the room.

"Let's see the money," the stubbled man said.

"Let's talk about what the money's for," Jackie
Brown said. "I want ten pieces, thirty-eights or better.
I want them now. The Duck says you have them."

"How long you know the Duck?" the stubbled man
said.

"Since I got grabbed at the Weirs about five years
ago and he was in the next cell with me," Jackie Brown
said.

"You still ride?" the stubbled man said.

"No," Jackie Brown said. "That was before I heard
about making money. I was just having fun then."

"You see any of the guys?" the stubbled man said.

"I saw some of them a couple years ago," Jackie
Brown said. "I happened to be up around here doing a
little business, and I see a lot of hogs around this place
outside town, so I stop, pass the time of day, and it
turns out to be Lowell, they got a charter, finally. The
big fellow was supposed to be in town."

"He was," the stubbled man said. "They had a coun-
cil of war."

"In the sand pit," Jackie Brown said. "Yeah, I know. Some of the Disciples and the Slaves, I heard they were looking to do some business with me, but I said, I sent the word back, no, I was through with that, and anyway, I was going to trade with anybody, and keep in mind I dunno which one you was with, I was to trade with anybody, I'd stay with the Angels. All of my friends, the guys I knew that stayed with it, they're with the Angels, and you don't, you know, you don't go back on that."

"You do any business?" the stubbled man said.

"Hey look," Jackie Brown said, "now why don't you put that fucking thing down so we can talk. I'm in kind a hurry. I got to see a man a good bit south of here and I want to get some goddamned supper some time tonight. No, I didn't sell nothing to the Angels. The kind of stuff I handle is sidearms, not like that piece you got there. The Angels didn't want any of that, that stuff I was trading."

The stubbled man pushed the safety on the shotgun. He lowered it, but kept it in his hands. "I think I can probably get you the ten," he said. "It'll be five bucks and I got to warn, the stuff is very hot. And we got to take a ride for it. Cash in front."

"Cash in front," Jackie Brown said. He produced his wallet and removed a packet of fifty-dollar bills. He counted off ten of them.

"Haven't you got anything smaller?" the stubbled man said.

"No," Jackie Brown said. "It's American money. Besides, you wouldn't want no tens or twenties anyway. There's a hell of a lot of bogus flying around in tens and twenties. Fifties're nice and safe. How much of a ride?"

"About an hour," the stubbled man said. "Grace, I'm going out. I'll be back."

"Which direction?" Jackie Brown said.

"Why?" the stubbled man said.

"Because if it's south I'd take my car and follow you," Jackie said. "I already told you, I got to go back the other way tonight."

"You're not taking no car," the stubbled man said. "We'll go in my car. Never mind where we're going. Come on, out the back way."

"Jesus Christ," Jackie Brown said, "by the time I get fucking home tonight, it'll be morning."

IN DESI'S PLACE on Fountain Street in Providence, Jackie Brown found a kid with greasy brown hair and a bad complexion. He was wearing a cheap, plaid sport shirt and chino pants and he needed a shave. He looked worried. He was sitting alone in a booth in the back of the restaurant.

Jackie Brown stopped at the table and said: "If I was telling you I was looking for a guy that was in the Marines with my brother once, you think you'd be able to help me?"

The kid's eyes filled with emotion. "I was getting worried," he said. "You were going to be here at seven-thirty. I had three plates of eggs so far."

"You should lay off the eggs," Jackie Brown said. "They make you fart worse'n beer."

"I like eggs," the kid said. "Especially, what I mean is, all we get're them powdered ones, that're always scrambled. Every time I get liberty, I go out and have myself some eggs."

"You get your cookies too?" Jackie Brown said.

"Huh?" the kid said.

"Never mind," Jackie Brown said. "I didn't come fucking down here to talk about fucking eggs. I came down here to do something. Let's do it. Where do we go?"

"Look," the kid said, "I don't know if they're still there. I mean, it's almost ten o'clock and all. I didn't have no way to check with them. We're supposed to be there by eight-fifteen. I didn't know what to do."

"Have we got to drive some place?" Jackie Brown said.

"Sure," the kid said. "That was the plan. They let me off here to wait for you and they went, you know, and I take you there and we get there about eight-fifteen and take care of it. I mean, I understood that was the way we were going to do it. We're just late, is all. I'm only telling you, I don't know if they're still there. Only thing we can do is go see. It's not my fault."

"Where've we got to drive to," Jackie Brown said, "and don't tell me it's south of here."

"Well we have," the kid said. "We got to go down the road to where we were going to meet. That was the way we were going to do it."

"Christ," Jackie Brown said. "I been on the god-damned road all day. Well, come on."

The kid was very impressed with the Roadrunner. "How much did it cost you?" he said.

"Look, I don't know," Jackie Brown said. "I bought it about a year ago. Four grand or so, I guess."

"Has it got the magnum mill?" the kid said.

"Hemi," Jackie Brown said, "three-eighty-three hemi. It goes."

"How come you got the automatic?" the kid said. "I had one, I'd want the Hurst shifter in it."

"You wouldn't want it once you started buying clutches for it," Jackie Brown said. "You let that thing out a few times and pretty soon you got this loud noise in the scatter shield. Or else she misses a shift on you and you got valves coming up through the hood like bullets. The Torqueflite's good enough, you get a high-ratio rear end and positraction it, and she'll wind out pretty good. Where're we going?"

"Look," the kid said, "you take the freeway south. You want to, with this thing we can be there in about fifteen minutes."

"I don't want to," Jackie Brown said. "I get pinched tonight with what I'm carrying, I'll never see the sun shine again. Legal limit all the way."

"Shit," the kid said. "I always wanted to see what one of these things can do."

"Well I tell you," Jackie Brown said, "you get me, say, another twenty-five or thirty of these rifles and you can get one of your own and see for yourself. But I'm Mister Lawabiding tonight, and that's all there is to it."

The Roadrunner went off at the Warwick-Apponaug ramp of Interstate 495 and burbled through the quiet streets. "You go down here about a mile or so and when you're almost into East Greenwich, you take a left. You got to keep your eyes open, though, because it goes down by the water there and then you hook a hard right and go up a dirt road."

"Where the fuck're you taking me?" Jackie Brown said. The car lurched into a narrow street that twisted down a steep hill. Overhanging evergreen branches brushed the roof and sides of the car. The headlights covered the tops of the trees now and again as the car jounced. At the foot of the hill the road ended at a small red building and a series of yacht slips. Several small quahaug boats lay comfortably at anchor in the dark water.

"You take the right here," the kid said. "You go up about a hundred yards and you come to a clearing. That's where they are. It's a horse farm in back of here. You can rent horses and go riding."

Jackie Brown nosed the Roadrunner into the dirt

parking area in front of the red building. He shut off
the lights. He put the car into reverse and backed it
around. When he finished, the car was pointing up the
hill they had just descended. The moon reflected on the
water of the harbor. Jackie Brown put the transmission
in Park. He opened the window and let salt air into the
car. "Get out," he said.

"No," the kid said, "up the hill there."

"Right," Jackie Brown said. "Get out and go up the
hill there, and get your friends and the rifles, and come
back down here and we'll do business. Here, not there."

"Why?" the kid said.

"Because I think you need exercise," Jackie Brown
said. "I'm afraid of horses. I like the moonlight. And
I'm not so fucking stupid as to drive this car into the
woods to find two other guys with machineguns who
know I've got money. This life's hard, but it's harder if
you're stupid. Now you go and get them, and I'll be
waiting here. When you come back I'll tell you what to
do next. Move."

The kid got out and shut the door. Jackie Brown
reached over and locked it. From the glove compartment he removed a chrome-plated forty-five automatic.
He switched on the courtesy lights, checked the safety
on the automatic, worked the slide back and jacked a
round into the chamber. He released the slide and then
let the safety off. He put the pistol on the dashboard.
From under the dashboard he unclipped a chromium
spotlight. He plugged it into the cigarette lighter and
placed it on the dashboard next to the pistol. The hemi
muttered quietly. He could hear the small boats working against their lines. He stared carefully up the road.
Three figures came slowly into the moonlit parking

area. Two of them carried rifles. They approached uncertainly. Jackie Brown said: "That's far enough." He picked up the spotlight and pointed it at them. "The two of you there, hand the rifles to the guy that was with me. Then stand still."

The kid had trouble getting all of the rifles into his arms.

"Now you come over here to the car. When you get here, I'll open the trunk from inside here. Put the rifles in the trunk and shut it. Come up to the window here and I'll give you the money. You other guys stand nice and still. I got a forty-five on you every minute. Any funny stuff and I'll put a big hole in you."

The kid did as he was told. Jackie Brown pushed the button of the inside trunk release with his knee. He heard the trunk gulp open. He heard the rifles clunking into the compartment. "Shut the goddamned trunk," he said. He heard the trunk close. "Come up here and don't get in the way of the light."

The kid came up to the window. "Where's the ammo?" Jackie Brown said.

"Huh?" the kid said.

"Where's the fucking goddamned bullets?" Jackie Brown said. "I told you I could use five hundred rounds. Where the fuck is it?"

"Oh," the kid said, "we couldn't get no ammo."

"You couldn't get any," Jackie Brown said. "You can steal the goddamned guns right out of Stores, but you can't get any bullets. What the hell do I do with guns and no bullets? I can't get that stuff outside."

"Look," the kid said, "we'll get it for you, honest. It's just, the kid that was going to get the ammo for us, he got sick and he wasn't on duty there when we come up.

We didn't want to take no chances getting it from somebody that maybe we couldn't be sure was all right."

"All right," Jackie Brown said. "I'm gonna be nice to you. Here's the whole five hundred for the guns. I oughta keep back a couple hundred for this putting me in the ditch with the ammo. But fuck it, my big weakness is I'm a nice guy. Now you get the rest of the stuff and you call me, okay?"

"Okay," the kid said. "Thanks a lot."

"And lay off them fucking eggs," Jackie Brown said. "They'll get you before you're through."

14

FOLEY AND WATERS sat in the chief's office with their feet on his desk and his television murmuring the tail end of the David Frost Show.

"I appreciate you waiting around, Maury," Foley said. "I didn't expect to have to see you today, but then I got the call and after I talked to him, I decided I better come in."

"It's all right," Waters said. "My wife keeps telling me I shouldn't do this, hang around government property after regular working hours, but I figure, hell, I'm supposed to catch the goddamned kids with their bombs. Only fair to give them a sporting shot at me, isn't it?"

"Look," Foley said. "I got to get clear of this junk detail once and for all. There's something going on with Eddie Fingers. The guy's all over the place all of a sudden, first he's seeing me, then I get this today that he's playing games with Scalisi. First it's the brothers and now it's the wise guys, and in the meantime I don't hear from him. I think I better be around for a while. This could turn into something."

"You check out the Panthers on that?" Waters said.

"Shit," Foley said, "I called old reliable Deetzer, who else've I got to call? He doesn't know anything, he told me so. I been telling Chickie Leavitt for at least a year we had to get somebody in there, and we don't because we won't spend the fucking money. The Deetzer knows about as much about what's going on as I do, only he's honest and admits it."

"The Bureau's supposed to have something in there," Waters said.

"Did we call the Bureau?" Foley said. "No, I bet. Nobody got around to it."

"We called the Bureau," Waters said. "I did it myself. They didn't know anything about it. They said they'd look into it."

"And thank you very much for calling," Foley said. "How about SP, they doing anything?"

"Everything copacetic as far as they know," Waters said. "Boston PD, the same. I think Coyle was jerking you off."

"I think so, too," Foley said. "What I want to know is, what the fuck is he up to? That bastard, he's about this high in the bunch, but he gets around more'n any man I ever see. One day he's here and the next day he's there, you'd think he was a fucking stray dog. I wish I had a line on half of what he's doing."

"Does he work anywhere?" Waters said.

"Yeah," Foley said, "he's an expediter over at Arliss Trucking, night expediter, but you just try to find him there. He works about as much as Santa Claus."

"Arliss Trucking," Waters said, "now where have I heard that one before?"

"It's in eight or ten files," Foley said. "It's a goddamned front for the boys. They all get reportable income from Arliss, and none of them work there. That company hires more people on less business than I ever see. They're the owners of record for about nine Lincoln Connies and at least four Cads. The Kraut spotted Dannie Theos the other day in a big maroon Bird and ran the number, it's registered to Crystal Ford, lease card, rented to Arliss Trucking."

The Frost Show ended and the news began. The announcer said: "In Wilbraham, early today, four gunmen burst into the home of a young bank officer, terrorized his family, and compelled him to hand over the contents of the vault at the Connecticut River Bank and Trust Company branch in that town. Officials estimated the take in excess of eighty thousand dollars, noting that the robbery was almost identical to one committed last Monday at the First Agricultural and Commercial Bank and Trust Company in Hopedale. The FBI has been called in on the case, and a full-scale investigation is underway."

"Did Scalisi ever operate that way?" Waters said.

"I don't know much about Scalisi," Foley said, "you want the honest to God's truth. My friend says Scalisi's been awful busy lately, can't stay at one phone long enough for anybody to call him back there. But I thought Scalisi was pretty much of a hit man, didn't do much of anything else."

"They branch out," Waters said.

"I know it," Foley said. "My friend there, he runs a saloon, and I know fucking well he's got an undisclosed interest, and he knows I know. But he's sure to have all kinds of other action going that I never dreamed of, let alone owning the saloon. He's a strange guy. I bet I talked to him a hundred times, and I couldn't tell you how much good stuff he's given me. I'm always handing him twenty, and he's always poor-mouthing me, and yet I know he's got something cooking all the time, you can feel it. It's like you're in a movie, and the other guy's in the movie with you, but he *knows* you're both in a movie, and what comes next. And you don't. I get the feeling, all the time, he's playing me."

"What do you think he's doing?" Waters asked.

"It's hard to say," Foley said. "What he's doing with me, that's easy. He's keeping a hook in. If he gets grabbed, he's going to come around to me and say: 'Hey, I need some help. I helped you. Are you a stand-up guy or not.' But half the stuff I get from him is stuff I get by listening to what he says, he doesn't know what he's telling me. And the other half, well, it's usually about somebody else, somebody that he doesn't like, maybe, or somebody that put the hammer on him and he's looking to get back. I'm almost certain he was in on the Polack hit, I could stake my life on it. I saw him the other day, a few days ago, I hadn't seen him for a long time, and I said to him: 'We still friends, Dillon?' This was right after I see Eddie Fingers that time in the plaza. And he starts this long involved riga-marole about how he's scared, he can't talk to me, he can't go to the grand jury for me, the town's buttoned up. Now the only grand jury I know about is the DA's, and that's about the Polack hit and they got that other fellow there, I hear, Stradniki, Stradnowski?"

"Stravinski," Waters said, "Jimmy the Whale."

"The Polack," Foley said, "yeah, him. They got the other Polack. And I'm not interested in that case, for Christ sake. They hit the Polack two years ago, it's nothing concerns me. But my friend's all uptight about it, he's so relieved when I start asking about something else it's like he finally took a piss after four days of drinking beer. Which is how I pick up what I got on this other matter, he gave me that for nothing, really, he was so relieved I wasn't pushing him."

"Who else was on that job," Waters said, "the Polack job?"

"A bunch of other tailgaters," Foley said. "I assume so, anyway. The Polack never did anything but steal, but he started getting lazy. You remember, they got away with about a hundred thou worth of stuff off Allied Storage, and then somebody stole it from the guys that stole it. The Combat Zone sounded like a war was going on there for a while, and the Polack turned up dead in the trunk of a Mercury in Chelsea. I heard Artie Van, for one."

"There's an interesting guy," Waters said. "I always thought Artie Van did a lot more'n he got credit for."

"A real shadowy character," Foley said. "From what I hear, a genuine stand-up guy. Until he gets in jail. Then people start to fret. But hard as nails and fish hooks while he's on the street. I hear they used to call up from Providence whenever they had a particularly bad piece of work and get ahold of Artie Van to carry the mail. But it's just what I hear."

"You hear anything about Artie Van and Jimmy Scalisi?" Waters said.

"Not together, no," Foley said.

"I was wondering," Waters said, "you suppose Van and Scalisi're making these withdrawals from banks?"

"It's a thought," Foley said. "I just wonder where Eddie Coyle fits in."

"Suppose Eddie Coyle was the armorer," Waters said. "I'm just thinking out loud, now."

"Hard to figure," Foley said. "Coyle's a small-timer. A colossal pain in the ass, of course, but basically a small-timer. I don't see how he'd get in there. I could check into it."

"Why don't you do that," Waters said. "I'll call Drugs and tell them I got to pull you off for a couple more weeks. They'll understand, I'm sure."

15

JACKIE BROWN brought the Roadrunner slowly into the Fresh Pond Shopping Center, chose a place in the middle of a row of cars, and killed the engine. He looked at his watch. It read two-fifty-eight. He opened the glove compartment and removed a tape cassette. He put it into the tape deck. Johnny Cash began to sing about Folsom Prison.

At five minutes past three Jackie Brown was dozing. The stocky man rapped on the window. Jackie Brown swung his head around. The stocky man had a cart full of shopping bags. He motioned to Jackie Brown to get out of the car.

"Where are they?" the stocky man said.

"In the trunk," Jackie Brown said.

"They in anything?" the stocky man said.

"A box," Jackie Brown said. "A big box with some newspapers in it."

"Okay," the stocky man said. "I got an extra bag here. Take it. Then we go around to the trunk and you open it. I'll put some of these bags in so it'll look like I was getting groceries for you. You put the guns in the bag and put the bag in the cart. Nobody'll pay any attention at all."

"Where's the money?" Jackie Brown said.

"Right here," the stocky man said. He handed over six hundred dollars in tens and twenties.

"This the genuine?" Jackie Brown said.

"If it isn't," the stocky man said, "you get in touch

with me and I'll call my banker. Far as I know it's the McCoy. You want to count it?"

"No," Jackie Brown said. "I haven't got much time. I'm supposed to be at the Route 128 railroad station at four-thirty. Let's get going."

"Fine with me," the stocky man said. He pulled the shopping cart back to the trunk.

"What's in the fucking bags?" Jackie Brown said.

"Three of them're full of bread," the stocky man said. "The rest've got meat and potatoes and some beer and vegetables, that kind of thing."

"What're you giving me?" Jackie Brown said.

"The bread," the stocky man said. "Man can always use a little bread. You can feed the goddamned pigeons or something. Go find some squirrels. Squirrels love bread."

"Your wife make you do the shopping too?" Jackie Brown said.

"My friend," the stocky man said, "you don't have much time and I'm kind of in a hurry myself. I don't have time to explain married life to you, and besides, you wouldn't believe me anyway. I didn't believe it when they told me, and you wouldn't believe it if I told you. Let's stick to business."

Jackie Brown opened the trunk. Inside there was a cardboard box which appeared to be filled with newspapers. The five M-sixteens lay across it.

"Jesus," the stocky man said.

"Don't get your bowels in an uproar," Jackie Brown said, "those're for somebody else. Your stuff's in the box, like I said."

"For Christ sake get it in the bag and hurry," the

stocky man said, "those look like fucking Army rifles to me."

"Well," Jackie Brown said, "they're military."

"Machineguns?" the stocky man said.

"Machineguns," Jackie Brown said. "The only thing that's more of a machinegun is the Colt, the AR-fifteen. But these're pretty good. Want to see one?"

"No," the stocky man said. "Fill the goddamned bag." He began lifting bags of bread into the trunk.

Jackie Brown put the shopping bag of sidearms in the cart. "You set now?" he said.

"Why'nt you put a couple loaves that bread on them," the stocky man said. "Case anybody gets curious."

Jackie Brown put two loaves of batter-whipped Sunbeam on top of the revolvers. "You got nine thirty-eights and one three-fifty-seven there," he said. "Good stuff, too. I hope you appreciate what I did for you."

"My friend," the stocky man said, "your name is in that great golden book up in the sky. I'll be in touch."

Jackie Brown watched the stocky man push the cart down the parking lot, then disappear behind a truck. Jackie Brown shut the trunk of the Roadrunner and got into the car. He started the engine. When he passed the truck, the stocky man was straightening up from the trunk of an old Cadillac. His legs hid the license plate. Jackie Brown waved. The stocky man made no sign of recognition. "I suppose I'll hear about that," Jackie Brown said. "I suppose I will."

16

EDDIE COYLE put his hands in his pockets and rested his back against the green metal post that supported the arcade of the shopping plaza above the telephone booths. Two women moved their lips as though deliberating over every single word of the hundreds they seemed to be uttering. A small man in a gold polo shirt stood with a receiver against his ear and a resigned expression on his face. From time to time he said something.

The man emerged first. "I'm sorry it took so long," he said.

"Think nothing of it," Eddie Coyle said. "Mine's the same way." The man grinned.

In the telephone booth, Eddie Coyle deposited a dime and dialed a Boston number. He said: "Foley there?" He paused for an instant. "No, I don't care to give my name. Gimme Foley and quit horsing around." He paused again. "Dave," he said, "I caught you in. Good. Whaddaya mean, who is this. We got mutual friends up in New Hampshire. This is Eddie. Yeah. Remember you wanted a strong reason? Yeah. Here it is: at four-thirty this afternoon, a kid in a metallic blue Roadrunner, Massachusetts registration number KX4-197, is going to meet some people at the 128 railroad station. He's going to sell them five M-sixteen machineguns. The guns're in the trunk of the Roadrunner." Coyle paused again. "KX4-197," he said, "Roadrunner, metallic blue. The kid's about twenty-six. About a hundred and sixty. Black hair, fairly short.

Sideburns. Suede jacket. Levi's, blue Levi's. Brown suede boots with fringe on them. Wears sunglasses a lot." Coyle paused again. "I dunno who he's going to sell them to. Perhaps if you was to go there, you could find out." Coyle paused again. "I imagine so," he said. "Now, you keep this in mind, okay? I came through." Coyle paused again. "You're welcome," he said, "always a pleasure to do a favor for a friend with a good memory."

Eddie Coyle replaced the handset in the receiver carefully. He opened the door of the booth and found a stout woman, about fifty, staring at him. "It took you long enough," she said.

"I was calling my poor sick mother," he said.

"Oh," she said, her face immediately relaxing into an expression of sympathy. "I'm sorry. Has she been ill long?"

Eddie Coyle smiled. "Fuck you, lady," he said, "*and the horse you rode in on.*"

JACKIE BROWN got caught in traffic in Watertown. He escaped briefly and got caught again in Newton. On 128, he eased the Roadrunner into a three-lane pack of first-shift electronics workers heading home, and settled down to an unobtrusive fifty miles per hour. There was a three-car accident in Needham, and he waited patiently in the center lane, surrounded by a thousand cars, while the sun declined and the evening began. At ten minutes past four he broke loose and resumed his fifty miles an hour. He took the ramp at the 128 railroad station at four-twenty-five. He proceeded at twenty miles an hour into the lot, looking for the tan Microbus. Not seeing it, he parked near the station. He opened the glove compartment and removed a cassette. He placed the cassette in the tape deck. Glen Campbell began to sing. Jackie Brown, his eyes red and puffed, slid down on the bucket seat and closed his eyes. In twenty-four hours he had driven nearly three hundred miles on four hours' sleep.

Dave Foley and Keith Moran sat in the green Charger, two parking lanes away. "We could take him now," Moran said.

"We could," Foley said. "We could also do what we're supposed to do, which is wait and see who comes up to buy the stuff. And that is what we are going to do."

At the entrance of the station, Ernie Sauter and Deke Ferris of the Massachusetts State Police, wearing sport

coats and slacks, conversed casually. Ferris had his
back to the Roadrunner. "What do you say?" he said.
"We could take him out right now."

"Yes," Sauter said, "and then Foley'd shoot us and
he'd be right. Calm the fuck down, will you?"

Six cars up the lane from Jackie Brown, a blue Sky-
lark convertible arrived and pulled in. The driver was
Tobin Ames. The passenger was Donald Morrissey.
"Foley here yet?" Morrissey said.

"I think that's him over there," Ames said. "The
green Charger. That him?"

"That's him," Morrissey said.

"Just keep an eye on him," Ames said. "I'll watch the
Roadrunner. When Foley moves, tell me."

The dusk was heavy at four-thirty-eight when the
tan Microbus came into the lot from the northbound
lane of 128. It turned up the first lane and came
down the second lane at perhaps ten miles per hour,
jerking along when the engine needed revs, speed-
ing up and then slowing down again. The curtains
shifted in the windows as the bus proceeded. It slowed
momentarily behind the Roadrunner, then moved
along to the next row. The driver found a space and
swung the bus in He got out of the left hand door. a
young man with long hair and a puffy face. He wore
a blue flannel shirt and a tan corduroy sport coat and
blue bib overalls and black boots. From the other door
emerged a thin girl, about twenty-two, with wispy
blonde hair cut short. She wore Levi's and a blue
denim shirt.

The two of them paused to talk behind the bus. Then
they walked toward the Roadrunner.

"Them ain't niggers," Tobin Ames said. "Them ain't niggers at all. Them's white folks."

"Oh shut up, Tobin," Morrissey said. "You bastards can't expect to have a man in every office." Morrissey's voice was somewhat choked. He had twisted his body in order to pick up two Remington short barrelled, twelve-gauge pump guns from the floor in the back. From his jacket, he took ten red double-O buckshot shells and started feeding them into the magazines.

In the Charger, Foley said: "Recognize them?"

"No, I don't," Moran said. "They look like student radicals, but then there's a whole mess of people that look like student radicals, that aren't, and another whole mess of people that don't look like radicals, but they sure are."

"These cats're after machineguns, remember," Foley said.

"That oughta qualify them," Moran said, "but I sure don't recognize them from anywhere. Bastards all look alike anyway." He and Foley sat with their shotguns cradled in their laps.

On the station platform, Ernie Sauter stood and watched the young man and the girl over Ferris' shoulder. "A couple of goddamned punks," he said. "Militants. You know, Deke, somebody's nuts. I don't know whether it's me or them, but somebody is definitely nuts. I just wished I knew, so I'd know, you know?"

The young man leaned over and knocked his knuckles against the window of the Roadrunner. Jackie Brown opened his left eye. Without any indication of haste, he cranked the window down.

"Yeah?" he said.

"Look," the young man said, "I hate like hell to bother you and all, but didn't we have some arrangement or something, we're supposed to meet here?"

"Yeah," Jackie Brown said.

"Well?" the young man said.

"Well, what?" Jackie Brown said.

"Are we going to do something?" the young man said.

"Sure," Jackie Brown said, "look around."

"Quit playing fucking games," the girl said. "What the hell is going on here? Why the hell did you bring us into a whole goddamn mob of people to sell machineguns? Is this some kind of a joke or something?"

"I'm a very cautious man," Jackie Brown said. "I plan to sit here for about two hours and maybe I'll nap a little. In the meantime, if every car I saw when I come in here doesn't leave, I'll know it. Around six-thirty, I'll know if you're trying to tip me in. If I know you're not, then I'll tell you something, and we'll go some place, and I'll give you some machineguns and you'll give me some money, and that'll be that."

"Did you drag us all the way out here for decoys?" the girl said.

"I do business by staying out of prison," Jackie Brown said. "I got five lifetimes in that trunk. I do anything I need to in order to stay out of prison. Within reason, of course. Now you just settle down. I been up all night and I can use a nap."

"We just stay here and sit?" the young man said.

"Look," Jackie Brown said, "I don't *care* what you do. I intend to stay here and take a nap, and wake up now and then. I'm not in the habit of swapping machineguns around in plain sight of everybody in the world. But it's a nice way to see if you got company, other people interested. You can stay or you can go. At six-thirty I'm leaving here and going some place else. You can wait around too, or you can go some place else now and come back around six thirty, and if everything's kosher, I'll tell you where we meet."

"Shit," the young man said.

"No," the girl said, "no, he's right. He's very right. I agree with him."

"Well, what the hell am I supposed to do?" the young man said, "sit here and get goddamned faint?"

"You could go get something to eat," Jackie Brown said. "There's a Ho-Jo about six miles back."

"Okay," the young man said, "so we eat. And then we come back. What happens then?"

"Right now, I don't know," Jackie Brown said. "If everybody that was here waiting for trains when I came in, isn't waiting for trains when you come back, we go some place and I sell you some machineguns. If there's somebody here then that was here when I came in, maybe we don't. If we do, we go out there and get into the traffic and you go south, or maybe north, and I go the other way, and we meet some place I haven't decided on yet, and you get some machineguns and I get some money."

"And some ammo," the girl said, "we get some ammo too."

"No you don't," Jackie Brown said. "I haven't got any ammo."

"You bastard," the girl said.

"I'm not going into that," Jackie Brown said. "I got you machineguns on short notice. I didn't get no ammo.

If I can get ammo, I will. I'm trying. But I haven't got any ammo right now. I'm working on it."

"Where're we going to get ammo?" the young man said.

"If I knew where you were going to get ammo," Jackie Brown said, "I'd get the ammo there myself and I'd have it for you now. I tell you I'm getting ammo for you. You can get it faster yourself, go get it. You want me to get it, you leave me alone to get it. I frankly don't give a rat's ass."

"This is a trick," the girl said.

"If you think it's a trick," Jackie Brown said, "you just go ahead and get in your goddamned bus and get the fuck out of here, no questions asked. You don't hurt me any. I got five machineguns and at least fifty people want to buy machineguns. You do what you like, you won't hurt my feelings. Around six-thirty I'm going to go some place else. You want to go there and get some machineguns, you come back here. Go think it over."

"The money," the young man said, "give us the money back."

"Fuck you," Jackie Brown said. "You made a deal. I'm still ready to go through with it. You want to back out, back out. No refunds."

"You cocksucker," the young man said.

"Leave it, Peter," the girl said. "Let's go and have something to eat. We can talk."

"Very sensible," Jackie Brown said. He cranked the window up and put his head back on the rest.

The young man and woman straightened up and walked away from the Roadrunner. They walked close together, talking. They returned to the Microbus and got inside. The brake lights came on and some blue smoke issued from the exhaust pipe. The bus pulled out of its parking place and started up the parking lane.

"Motherfucker," Foley said.

"Don't be so eager," Moran said. "Maybe they're coming down in back of his car."

The Microbus continued up the parking lane. It turned right at the top of the lane and headed toward the northbound ramp out of the station area.

"*Motherfucker*," Foley said.

"Think quick," Moran said, "before they get into that traffic. Is there *any*thing we can bust them on?"

"No," Foley said, "not a goddamned thing."

"All right," Moran said. "So we got two possibilities. He's still here. He looks like he's settling in. So we can wait until he leaves and bust him then."

"If he doesn't get into the traffic," Foley said.

"Right," Moran said. "Or we can wait and get lucky and they'll come back and we'll bust the whole bunch of them."

"Or they'll come back and they'll all go some place and we'll lose them in traffic," Foley said.

"Right," Moran said, "three alternatives. What do we do?"

"He isn't moving," Foley said. "He looks like he's sleeping to me. So we can wait. But if we blow it, five machineguns go into the movement or something, and how the hell do we account for that?"

"I dunno," Moran said, "how do we?"

"We don't," Foley said. "It looks to me like the deal fell through. We got enough to arrest him now, right?"

"Right," Moran said.

"Lemme think," Foley said.

"It's your party," Moran said.

"We take him," Foley said. He touched the emergency flasher button on the dashboard. The turn signals blinked four times in the heavy twilight.

On the station platform, Sauter and Ferris removed thirty-eight caliber Chief's Specials from their holsters. They put them in the pockets of their sport coats. Together they stepped off the platform and started up the parking lane in front of the Roadrunner and the line of cars that blocked it.

Tobin Ames hit the ignition of the Skylark and put it into reverse. He backed out of the parking place slowly, rotating the steering wheel to point the convertible down the lane.

Jackie Brown sat with his eyes shut, his head back on the rest.

Foley and Moran got out of the Charger. They put on raincoats. They reached into the Charger and pulled the shotguns out. They put the shotguns under their raincoats. Each inserted his right hand through the lining of his raincoat and held the shotgun flat against his body. They began walking toward the Roadrunner.

Foley and Moran paused while a small group of commuters walked past.

Behind the Roadrunner, Foley and Moran separated. Foley stayed put. Moran walked up two car-widths and stood still. Ferris and Sauter stood talking on the edge of the next lane.

Ames brought the Skylark slowly down the lane. He did not have his headlights on. A pedestrian said: "Hey, use your lights." Ames brought the Skylark creeping along.

When the Skylark was behind the Roadrunner, perhaps four feet away, Ames stopped. He put it in Park.

He opened the door and got out. He had the shotgun in his hands. Morrissey emerged from the passenger side, carrying a shotgun. He leaned against the door of the Skylark and held the shotgun across his body. Ames bent his body and rested his elbows on the hood of the Skylark. He leveled his shotgun.

Jackie Brown, his eyes closed, rested his head and napped.

Sauter and Ferris parted. Sauter stayed put, drawing his revolver and holding it at his side. He faced the Roadrunner from a slight angle off the left front fender. Ferris took a similar position on the right.

Two commuters stopped. "Hey," one said, "what's going on here?"

Tobin Ames, without moving, said: "Insurance cashed cheap. Move on. United States Treasury."

The commuters broke into a jog. They stopped five cars away. In the early evening the mist commenced over the swamps of Dedham. It showed in halos around the lamps.

Foley approached the Roadrunner from the left rear. Moran approached from the right rear.

Foley brought the shotgun out from under his rain-coat. He lifted it slowly to the level of the windowsill of the Roadrunner and silently rested it there.

Moran stepped back two paces from the Roadrunner. He tucked the stock of the shotgun in at his waist with his right elbow. With his left hand he gripped the pump action. He brought the muzzle up to point at the window.

Jackie Brown, with his eyes closed, recovered from a long night of driving, and many frustrations.

Foley knocked on the window of the Roadrunner.

Lazily, Jackie Brown turned his head. He opened his left eye. His gaze focused on the face of a stranger. "Yeah?" he said.

Foley made a cranking motion with his left hand.

Jackie Brown shook his head. He reached forward and rolled the window down. "Yeah?" he said again.

"United States Treasury," Foley said. "You're under arrest. Come out slow and easy and keep your hands in plain sight. One move and you're a dead fucking man." He brought the shotgun up with his right hand. He brought his left hand under the pump and held it steady.

"Holy shit," Jackie Brown said. He looked to his right. Moran stood there, pointing a shotgun through the window. In front of the Roadrunner, two men advanced with revolvers pointed at him through the windshield. "Hey," he said.

"Get out of the car," Foley said. He reached in and lifted the door lock. He opened the door from the outside. "Get out." The shotgun remained leveled at Jackie Brown's head.

"Hey," Jackie Brown said, swinging his legs out of the car, "Hey, look."

Foley grabbed him as he got out. Foley turned him around. "Put your hands on the roof of the car," Foley said. "Move your feet back."

Jackie Brown did as he was told. He felt hands begin to pat him down. "What the fuck's this all about?" he said.

Moran, Sauter and Ferris now came around the Roadrunner and stood together with their weapons pointing at Jackie Brown. Ames and Morrissey stayed put. Moran handed his shotgun to Sauter, who let the hammer down on his Chief's Special and leveled Moran's shotgun. Moran removed his wallet from his hip pocket. He extracted a plasticized card from the wallet. In the blue-tinged glare of the parking lot lights, he began to read:

" 'You are under arrest for violation of a federal law. Before we ask you any questions, we want you to understand your rights under the Constitution of the United States.' "

"I know my rights," Jackie Brown said.

"Shut the fuck up and listen," Foley said. "Shut your goddamned mouth and listen to what the man's telling you."

" 'You do not have to answer any questions,' " Moran said. " 'You have a right to remain silent. If you answer any questions, your answers may be used in evidence against you in a trial in a court of law. Do you understand what I have read to you?' "

"Of course I understand," Jackie Brown said. "You think I'm a fucking idiot?"

"Shut up," Foley said, "and hold still or I'll blow your fucking head off." He rested the barrel of the Remington on Jackie Brown's shoulder. The muzzle grazed the base of Jackie Brown's skull.

" 'You are entitled to the advice of counsel,' " Moran said. " 'Do you have a lawyer?' "

"No, for Christ sake," Jackie Brown said. "Of course I don't. I just got arrested."

" 'If you want a lawyer,' " Moran said, " 'You need only say so, and you will be given time to engage a lawyer, and to confer with him. You are entitled to confer

with your lawyer before you decide whether to answer
any questions. Do you understand what I have read to
you?'"

Jackie Brown did not answer. Foley jabbed him with
the muzzle of the Remington. "Tell him," he said.

"Of course I understand," Jackie Brown said.

"'If you can't afford a lawyer,'" Moran said, "'the
court will appoint one for you. Do you understand
that?'"

"Yes," Jackie Brown said.

"'You may, if you wish, waive these rights and
answer our questions. Are you willing to answer questions?'" Moran said.

"Fuck, no," Jackie Brown said.

"Do you understand your rights?" Moran said.

"Yes," Jackie Brown said, "yes, yes, yes."

"Shut up," Moran said. "Turn around and hold out
your wrists." Foley snapped handcuffs on Jackie
Brown's wrists. "You're under arrest for violation of
U.S. Code twenty-six, Section fifty-eight-sixty-one, possession of a machinegun without being registered as
the owner and possessor of a machinegun."

"Hey," Jackie Brown said.

"Shut up," Foley said. "I don't want to hear one more
fucking word out of you. You keep your goddamned
trap shut. Now get in your car. In the back seat. Moran,
get in with him and keep the son of a bitch covered. If
he moves, blow his head off."

From his raincoat pocket, Foley removed a Citizen's
Band transmitter. He switched it on. "Tell him," he
said, "tell him we got the man in the place where he
was supposed to be, and tell him we want a warrant to
search the goddamned car. We're coming in."

"You knew it," Jackie Brown said, "you knew it. You knew I was going to be here."

"Sure," Foley said, getting into the Roadrunner. "Ames," he said, "have Morrissey bring my car in. Keys under the seat. What else," he said to Jackie Brown.

"That fucking bastard," Jackie Brown said, "that fucking bastard."

"What fucking bastard?" Moran said.

Jackie Brown looked at him. "Oh no," he said, "oh no. I'll settle that myself."

 **18**

IN A DEPLETED sandpit in Orange, Massachusetts, there is a trailer park. In the darkness, Eddie Coyle drove the old Sedan de Ville cautiously, the quad headlights on high beam, the oversized tires lapping over the edges of the narrow blacktop. He stopped the car beside an aqua and yellow trailer. It was equipped with wrought iron railings and flimsy iron steps; there was a heavy silver fabric wrapped around the undercarriage. The windows of the trailer were curtained. Light glowed behind them.

Eddie Coyle shut off the lights and the engine of the Cadillac. He got out and walked stiffly to the steps. He rang the doorbell without climbing the steps.

The curtain at the door window moved slightly. A woman peered out through the condensation on the glass. Eddie Coyle waited patiently. The door opened partway.

"Yes?" she said.

"I brought some groceries for Jimmy," Eddie Coyle said.

"Is he expecting you?" she said.

"I dunno," Coyle said. "He told me to come up here and all. I just drove about two hours. I hope so."

The woman said: "Just a minute." The door closed. Eddie Coyle waited in the chill dark.

The door opened partway again. A pocked male face appeared. "Who is it?" its voice said.

"Coyle," Eddie Coyle said. "I brought the groceries."

The door opened all the way. Jimmy Scalisi, wearing

a tee-shirt and a pair of gray pants, stood in the light. "Hey, Eddie," he said, "okay. Whyn't you bring the stuff in. I'd help you, but I'd freeze my ass off out there."

"It's okay," Coyle said. He returned to the Cadillac. He opened the trunk. He removed shopping bags, two at a time, and delivered them to Scalisi at the door of the trailer. There were six of them.

"Come on in," Scalisi said. Coyle followed him into the trailer. "This is Wanda," Scalisi said.

Wanda was five-ten, a hundred and thirty pounds. She had heavy breasts which Coyle noticed immediately because she was wearing a tee-shirt and a bra with bright red flowers. She was also wearing wheat-colored jeans. There were noticeable stains at the crotch. "Hi," she said.

"What do you do?" Coyle said.

"She works for Northeast," Scalisi said.

"I'm a stewardess," she said.

"Yes indeed," Coyle said. Wanda smiled.

"What's in the bags," Scalisi said.

"Meat and beer and stuff," Coyle said. "Now you mention it, I could use a beer."

"Wanda," Scalisi said, "Get the man a beer. We'll be inna living room."

In the living room of the trailer there was a black leather chair and a couch. Scalisi took the chair. Coyle sat gratefully on the couch. A portable color television stood on the counter between the living room and the dining area. The sound was off. A man was mouthing words and holding up a brochure about Hawaii.

"This is pretty nice," Coyle said. "I been on ice once or twice, but never as nice as this."

"I'm not on ice," Scalisi said. "I lived here two and a half years."

"Shit," Coyle said.

"No," Scalisi said. "I rent this place. I'm a bulldozer driver. I got seasonal work. The owner understands. He thinks I'm the greatest thing since sliced bread."

"Your wife understand?" Coyle said.

"What you don't know," Scalisi said, "it doesn't bother you. She don't know."

"She thinks you're off selling magazines," Coyle said.

"I dunno what she thinks," Scalisi said, "I told her I hadda go away for a while. She don't question it."

"Jesus," Coyle said, "I got to talk to you some time. I don't know how you do it."

"It's confidence," Scalisi said. "You look them right in the eye and say: Hey, I gotta go away for a while. They'll buy it."

"You got to meet my wife," Coyle said. "You said that to my wife, you was me, she'd get this look on her face. Oh yeah? Like you was trying to sell her a used car. I got to take the time and watch you. That's the only way."

Scalisi laughed.

Coyle indicated the kitchen area by moving his head. "That's pretty nice, too," he said, "where'd you get that?"

"Oh, you know," Scalisi said. "I'm over at Arliss one night and one of the guys comes in with her. We more or less strike up a conversation. One of those things."

Coyle rubbed his crotch.

"Very warm there," Scalisi said. "She don't wear no pants. I ask her why and she says she don't own no pants. Wears them panty hose when she's working. She gets in them dungarees, no pants. Now and then I just come up behind her and reach right down here. She comes off like she was on electricity. I never see anything like it."

"Jesus," Coyle said.

"It's a great life," Scalisi said, "if you don't weaken, it's a great life."

"So what're you doing?" Coyle said.

"Well," Scalisi said, "I was watching the Broons. They got a great club there. That's one problem with being in the construction business. You got to come up here. Can't go to no Broons games. I sort of miss that."

"Hey, look," Coyle said, "you're better off. I was over at the stadium there, well, you remember, and I was thinking, you got a lousy game on the tee-vee, you know, well, you just shut it off and go do something else. I was talking to Joey there, yesterday it was, down at Dillon's, he was at that Seals game, and he said, Jesus, it was fucking awful, but you paid for the seat, you know? They got to thinking they can beat the other guys throwing their clippings onna rink, and there you are, well, you paid for the seat, you aren't gonna *leave*, you know."

"I know," Scalisi said. "I still miss the guys. You go down there and have a squid or something and then you go to the game, it's nice, you know? It's a nice time. I kind of like it."

"Most of the girls down there wear pants," Coyle said.

"Hey, now," Scalisi said, "I know that. I mean, I'm not knocking it, you know? But I was just saying, I miss it."

"Things're going pretty good," Coyle said.

"Very nice," Scalisi said. "Things're going very nice. Arthur's good and careful. Yeah, very nice. You bring the stuff?"

"Out in the kitchen," Coyle said. "I put it under the chair. Right inna shopping bag, under the chair. All set."

"You done all right on this one," Scalisi said. "I want you to know, I appreciate it. I been able to talk some sense to Arthur, you know, about hanging onto the stuff. He starts getting all bothered and I just say: 'Well, Arthur, you know, Eddie's done all right by us so far. He'll have some more. Now heave it inna god-damned river.' Damn near breaks his heart," Scalisi said. "You can see he doesn't want to do it. Arthur gets a good piece, he hates to part with it. But he does it. And it makes a difference, you know? It's a lot safer, knowing nobody's going around with a piece on him, case he gets picked up on suspicion. It really makes a difference."

Wanda came in with a tray. It held a quart of beer and two glasses. "That's pretty nice meat you brought," she said. "I was putting it away there, and I looked it over."

"Hey, thanks," Scalisi said. "How much I owe you for the groceries?"

"Well, let's see," Eddie Coyle said. "Twelve for the first batch, the eight. Then there was another dozen, eighteen bucks for that. Now there's ten here, another fifteen hundred. Forty-five hundred. I'll throw in the steaks."

"My God," Wanda said, "that's a lot of money for some meat."

"Shut up, Wanda," Scalisi said.

"You know my friend here, I think," she said, "very large gangster type."

"I told you," Scalisi said, "shut up."

"Fuck you," Wanda said. "I heard you talking about me, I was out there, I heard you. What business of his is it, I wear pants or not. What am I, something you brag about? My kid brother talks about his goddamned Mustang the same way you talk about me. 'I just reach down there every so often and set her off.' For Christ sake. I thought we were friends. I thought we liked each other. Shit."

"You got this trouble?" Scalisi said to Coyle.

"Yeah," Coyle said, "different, but the same. Hasn't everybody?"

"Fuck you too," Wanda said to Coyle.

"I think it's all this Women's Lib stuff or something," Scalisi said. "I'll be Christ if I know what to make out of it."

"I don't think they got enough on their minds," Coyle said. "You know, hacking around all day. They stand around there thinking, you get home and they're all pissed off and all you did was put the goddamned car in the yard. They need some good worries, is what I think."

"I work," Wanda said, "I probably work more'n both of you bastards put together. I earn my keep."

"I told you to shut up," Scalisi said.

"I told you to go and fuck yourself," Wanda said. "Talking about me like that. How'd you like it if I was to start telling the girl at the store about your prick and what you like me to do with it? With me, the things you like to do with me, would you like that?"

Scalisi came out of the chair quickly and slapped

Wanda across the face. "I told you to shut up," he said. "That's what I want you to do. Shut fucking up."

"No," she said. She did not cry. "No, you wouldn't like that. And you better sleep with both eyes open tonight, because maybe I'll decide to hit you with a hammer, you bastard."

Wanda stamped out of the living area and made as much noise as she could shutting the folding door to the sleeping area.

"You ever get laid," Scalisi said.

"Sure," Coyle said.

"You ever get laid without a lot of goddamned *talk*?" Scalisi said. "That's really what I mean. I'm beginning to understand the guys, that go down to the hotel and pick something out and pay twenty bucks. I really mean it. You pays your money and you say: 'Blow me.' And she blows you. No crap, you don't get a load of shit about it. It's clean and you can see what you're doing. I used to think, well, any man's got to pay for it, he might as well cut it off, you know? But the old lady's whining and bitching all the time and then I get this wired up and I think, well, all right, here's something and there isn't any talking and stuff, you know? I been with this broad for probably a year and a half. And I *know* she's screwing whoever says please and thank you on the plane to her, and *I* don't care. I mean, what the hell, I'm not perfect. It isn't as though she come walking into it blind and stupid, you know? But what does she do? She's mad because I tell the goddamned truth. She *don't* wear no pants. That's obvious. You take a look at her, you know. So where's the thing, I mean? What harm does it do? The broad's great in the sack and she lights off real easy. So I say it, and now she's mad. I don't know."

"Look," Coyle said, "they're all batty. I come home the other night, I hit the number. I got six hundred and fifty bucks on me. Six hundred and fifty bucks. I'm thinking about buying her a color tee-vee. She watches the fucking thing all the time. I figure she'll enjoy it. So what happens? I come in the door. What does she say: 'Where the hell've you been? The oil burner's all smoky and I can't get the repairman.' So right there I forget about the color tee-vee. I went out in the morning and I come home at night and she's pissed off. Screw her. I went out and opened a fucking bank account. *In my name.* Next February or so I'm gonna have some business down in Miami, there, and I'm gonna get warm. To hell with her."

"Hey," Scalisi said, "the money. How much?"

"Forty-five hundred," Coyle said.

"I'll be right with you." Scalisi got up again and left the living area. In a few minutes he returned. He had a packet of bills. He handed it to Coyle. "Count it," he said.

"No," Coyle said. He accepted the packet and put it in his pocket. "No, you never screwed me yet. I trust you." He got up.

"You gotta go?" Scalisi said.

"I got a long ride," Coyle said. "You got something else on your mind anyway. You gonna need any more guns?"

"I don't think so," Scalisi said. "Look, I'll let you know. I think we're just about finished. You gonna be around?"

"At least until next month," Coyle said. "I got that thing in New Hampshire coming up. I don't know."

"That gonna be a problem?" Scalisi said.

"I don't know," Coyle said. "I'm waiting to hear. Maybe not. Hell, how do you know? It comes, it comes. You take it the way it comes. I don't know."

"I hope you're all right," Scalisi said.

"Me too," Coyle said, "me too."

WITH NO EXPRESSION on his face, Jackie Brown sat in the outer office, his cuffed hands in his lap. Tobin Ames, a shotgun across his lap, sat behind a desk, opposite Jackie Brown, watching him. In the chief's office, Waters and Foley watched Ames and Jackie Brown through the glass partition.

"Did he say anything?" Waters said.

"He said he understood his fucking rights," Foley said. "He's a tough kid, I'll say that for him."

"When did you arrest him?" Waters said.

"About quarter of five," Foley said.

"I guess you stopped off for a drink on the way in," Waters said.

"You ever been in that traffic on Route 128?" Foley said. "We brought him up to the marshal's office and mugged him and printed him and then we brought him here."

"Okay," Waters said. "Now it's almost eight-thirty. You got some plans for him for the rest of the evening, I hope."

"Sure," Foley said. "We're gonna charge him."

"Good," Waters said. "I think that's an excellent idea. You got any idea of what you're going to charge him with?"

"Yeah," Foley said, "Twenty-six, fifty-eight-sixty-one. Possession of unregistered machineguns. Five of them."

"Well," Waters said, "what're you waiting for, Easter? I mean, you had him for almost four hours. He oughta be charged."

"I know he oughta be charged, Maury," Foley said, "but I don't make warrants out of thin air. Moran had to get a search warrant for the car. Then we searched it. We found the guns. Now Moran's getting a complaint. I got a Commissioner all lined up. Soon as Moran gets the complaint, off we go."

"I had tickets for the Bruins game tonight," Waters said.

"Hey," Foley said, "look, I know, I'm sorry. I just thought I oughta talk to you."

"So talk," Waters said.

"What do I do now?" Foley said.

"You mean after you get him bailed and so forth," Waters said. "That's the first thing you do."

"I know," Foley said. "But then what?"

"What're the choices?" Waters said.

"Okay," Foley said. "I can let him go. The Commissioner's sure to let him go in personal security. I can say: 'Okay, Mister Brown, see you in court.' And then try to get an indictment on the son of a bitch."

"You think you're going to get one?" Waters said.

"I think so," Foley said. "That bastard in the U.S. Attorney's office, I don't think even he can find anything wrong with this one. I did everything I could think of, and Moran thought of some other stuff. I tell you, if this kid wanted to take a leak, I'd get a warrant before I'd let him do it."

"Okay," Waters said, "you can let him go and indict him. What else?"

"I could say something to him before he goes," Foley said.

"Like what?" Waters said.

"Well," Foley said, "for example, he knows somebody

tipped us. He's not stupid. He figured out we got word he was going to be over at the railroad station. Couple times, driving in, he said: 'Who told you? Who told you I was going to be there?' "

"You wrote that down, I hope," Waters said.

"I wrote it down," Foley said.

"Okay," Waters said, "he was asking questions. So what?"

"So suppose we tell him?" Foley said.

"Tell him what?" Waters said.

"Well," Foley said, "we got a choice. We could let him think the kids in the VW bus did it."

"He going to believe that?" Waters said.

"Probably not," Foley said. "He might, but probably not."

"So why do it?" Waters said.

"To get their names," Foley said. "I'm not saying this is what we ought to do. I'm just saying, we could."

"You get the license number on the bus?" Waters said.

"Yeah," Foley said.

"Sooner or later that's going to tell us who was in it, right?" Waters said.

"Likely," Foley said, "unless it's stolen."

"Assume it's not," Waters said, "what have we got?"

"The names," Foley said.

"And for evidence we can show they drove the bus to the railroad station," Waters said. "Is that a federal crime, to drive a bus to the railroad station?"

"To buy machineguns, sure," Foley said.

"Who's going to say that?" Waters said.

"Jackie Brown," Foley said.

"Suppose he doesn't," Waters said.

"Nobody," Foley said. "Nobody in the world."

"You still got a federal crime?" Waters said.

"Sure," Foley said.

"Sure," Waters said, "but you can't prove it, is all."

"Right," Foley said.

"Next question," Waters said.

"I could tell him Coyle tipped us," Foley said.

"That's an interesting notion," Waters said. "Why tell him that?"

"It'd make him mad," Foley said. "I'm reasonably sure he was up to something with Coyle. So I tell him Coyle blew the whistle, he gets mad and tells me what he was doing with Coyle."

"Is it worth it?" Waters said.

"Well," Foley said, "you told me yourself, suppose Coyle was arming those bank robbers. If he was, maybe Jackie Brown was peddling the guns to him."

"You'd like those bank robbers," Waters said.

"Yes indeed," Foley said, "mighty fine."

"Okay," Waters said, "you tell Brown. Then what happens."

"I dunno," Foley said.

"I do," Waters said, "he gets arraigned on charges of possessing unregistered machineguns. Then he gets turned loose. Then what."

"He goes looking for Coyle," Foley said.

"Sure," Waters said, "he goes looking for Coyle, and when he finds him, he kills him. Then what've you got? One machinegun salesman and one dead fink. Is that what you want?"

"Probably not," Foley said. "Is there any way I can hold him without bail?"

"No," Waters said. "The purpose of bail . . . do you want to hear the whole lecture?"

"No," Foley said. " 'To insure that the accused will appear for subsequent proceedings.' Even with machineguns?"

"Even with machineguns," Waters said.

"Okay," Foley said, "he gonna get out. I can still tell him."

"And then he's going to tell you?" Waters said.

"Probably not," Foley said. "He looks like the type that wouldn't tell you if your coat was on fire."

"So what's going to happen?" Waters said.

"He's going to go looking for Coyle," Foley said, "and I'm going to tail him."

"Come on," Waters said.

"I'll put a homing device in his car," Foley said. "I'll track him on a fucking radio."

"Just like *Mission Impossible*," Waters said.

"Efrem Zimbalist is my favorite," Foley said. "Just like the Effa-Bee-Eye."

"Remind me to get you transferred to Topeka," Waters said. "You got any other bright ideas?"

"Yeah," Foley said. "I can tell him it was the guy that sold him the guns."

"Now there's a thought," Waters said. "Let's explore that. Who was it?"

"Some young punk soldier, I bet," Foley said.

"Where'd he get the gun?" Waters said.

"It's probably his," Foley said. "Him and four buddies want a little dough to get a high class piece of tail."

"Numbers on them guns?" Waters said.

"Yup," Foley said.

"Serial numbers registered to the soldier who gets the gun?" Waters said.

"Yeah," Foley said.

"Soldier got to account for the gun when it turns up gone?" Waters said.

"Yeah," Foley said.

"What do we gain from that?" Waters said. "We're going to find out anyway."

"You win," Foley said. "I don't tell him it was the soldiers."

"And you don't tell him it was the people in the bus, and you don't tell him it was Coyle," Waters said.

"I don't tell him nothing," Foley said. "I let him go in personal surety."

"Then what happens?" Waters said.

"He hits the street," Foley said, "and I start trying to get that bastard in the courthouse to indict him."

"But what does he do?" Waters said.

"He goes home and thinks," Foley said.

"Right," Waters said, "stupid, he isn't. What does he think?"

"The first thing he thinks is whether the people in the bus dumped him," Foley said.

"Right," Waters said, "and what does he decide?"

"He decides, no," Foley said. "They were there, but they didn't know anything. He decides it wasn't them."

"Then what does he do?" Waters said.

"He starts thinking about who else could've dumped him," Foley said.

"Who's he gonna pick?" Waters said.

"Coyle, first," Foley said. "If he knows Coyle's name. He saw Coyle this afternoon, I'd bet on it. Coyle probably saw the machineguns. He's gonna blame Coyle."

"How'd Coyle see the machineguns?" Waters said.

"The kid opened the trunk," Foley said.

"Why would he open the trunk?" Waters said.

"To get something out of it for Coyle," Foley said. "Of course."

"Coyle bought himself some guns today," Waters said.

"Of course Coyle could've sold him the machineguns," Foley said.

"Where would Coyle get machineguns?" Waters said. "Army machineguns? No. Coyle was buying something."

"So he thinks it was Coyle and he goes looking for him," Foley said. "Now what can we do about that?"

"You think he knows who Coyle is?" Waters said.

"His name?" Foley said. "Maybe. Probably not. Maybe his first name. Not the rest of it. Who he fits with? Probably. He's a tough, smart kid. He probably started thinking Mafia, the minute Coyle went out for guns. Coyle ain't no Panther, that's for sure, and he's no revolutionary. The kid probably knows Coyle's a gangster."

"Okay," Waters said. "Now maybe we got something. The kid gets bailed and he wants to know who set up the grab, so he starts thinking, and he decides he got set up by the boys. If he's smart, he isn't going to go around shooting one of them, and he's smart. So he's gonna want to get even. Now, how can a fellow get even with one of the boys that set him up?"

"Well," Foley said, "he could call him up at all hours of the night and breathe at him."

"Yes," Waters said, "and he could poison the guy's water hole and put it out around town that the guy's wife's fucking somebody else. But there's an easier way, isn't there?"

"Certainly," Foley said. "One calls one's friendly law enforcement officer and finks on the bastard that finks on you."

"Exactly," Waters said. "Now, do you suppose you could think of something to say that would express to Jackie Brown the deep regret you feel personally at having to arrest him, and your sincere conviction that he was set up?"

"Leave me give it some thought," Foley said. "I always hated to see a kid taken advantage of."

"I know how you feel," Waters said.

"Particularly since we missed the revolutionaries," Foley said. "It's an ill wind that blows nobody."

20

ROBERT L. BIGGERS of Duxbury, having been unable to sleep, dawdled over breakfast and read the *Herald* thoroughly. His wife walked sleepily into the kitchen with the baby as he was getting his coat. "Your head hurt or something?" she said.

"No more'n usual," he said, "why?"

"You're up so early," she said. "I thought something was the matter."

"Nothing at all," he said, "I just thought, you know, it's the early bird that catches the worm. I get in early today, I can wrap up those Christmas Club promotions and maybe get home at a decent hour, for once."

"Have a good day," she said.

"I will," he said. He kissed her goodbye.

Robert Biggers locked his car and walked through the parking lot at the West Marshfield Shopping Plaza toward the principal office of the Massachusetts Bay Cooperative Bank. He used his key to open the front door of the bank. He locked the door behind him. He went directly to the coat closet, removing his trench-coat, and hung it up. He emerged from the ante-room, humming a Supremes song he had heard on his way to work. Facing him was a medium-sized man. The man wore an orange nylon ski parka and a nylon stocking mask. In his right hand the man held an enormous black revolver.

"What the fuck?" Robert Biggers said.

The man motioned to his own right with the revolver.

Robert Biggers said: "What the fuck are you doing here? What the fuck is going *on?*"

"Move," the man said.

In the branch officer's private office, Harry Burrell sat in his chair with his hands clasped across his stomach. There were two more men in the office with him. They wore orange nylon parkas and nylon stockings over their faces. Each of them had a black revolver.

"We're being held up, Bob," Harry said. "I hope you and the rest of the staff won't do anything courageous or foolish, which is much the same thing in these circumstances. These men have a friend with them. He's at my house with my wife, who is probably having hysterics by now. They've assured me they don't want to hurt anyone, they only want the money. You're to stay here until the normal opening time and then go about your business. When the time lock opens, they will take the money and leave. I will go with them. Just don't do anything to interfere with them, and everything will be all right."

"My God," Robert Biggers said.

"It's not all unusual," Harry Burrell said. "I've been in this business for thirty-six years. I've been held up, this is the fourth time. It's been my experience that people like this're generally telling the truth. They want the money. They don't want to hurt us. If we can keep calm, we'll be all right."

"None of this is happening," Robert Biggers said.

"I'm afraid it is," Harry Burrell said. "Just keep calm and everything will be all right. Now, I have something for you to do. Can you handle it?"

"Of course," Biggers said.

"Go out front," Harry Burrell said. "As the rest of the

people arrive, let them in. Close the door each time. Take them into the cloakroom and explain to them what's going on, and that they're not to do anything that would jeopardize anyone. Keeping in mind that my wife's under a gun at home. Can you do that?"

One of the men spoke. "Just keep everybody nice and easy," he said. "No commotion, no alarm, no nothing. That's what he wants you to do."

"I can do that," Robert Biggers said.

"Fine," Harry Burrell said. "You go ahead now, and remember, I'm relying on you."

Robert Biggers sat at his desk and made no pretense of working. His mind ran furiously, in no apparent direction. As the three tellers arrived he let them in, made the same explanation to each — "We're being robbed. They're waiting for the time lock to open. Don't make any noise, or do anything. There's another man with Mrs. Burrell, waiting." — and ushered them to the cloakroom.

Nancy Williams was the only one who did not react calmly. She was nineteen, just out of high school the previous June. Her eyes opened very wide. "You're kidding me," she said.

"No," he said.

"They're really here?" she said.

They were standing in the corridor next to the coat closet. One of the men with guns had padded up while they were talking. Nancy Williams turned around and stared into the black revolver. "Oh my *God*," she said.

Robert Biggers felt a surge of wrathful protectiveness. On three Thursday evenings, after eight o'clock closing, he had taken Nancy Williams to dinner at the Post House. He had purchased several drinks for her. Then he had taken her to the Lantern Lodge and undressed her and screwed the socks off her. She was young and firm, and her nipples came up fast under tweaking. "Hey," he said.

"Get to work, sweetie," the man said. He motioned with the gun again. "You too, Gene Autry. Never mind this hacking around in the coat closet."

Nancy Williams hesitated, then walked toward the tellers' cages.

"Nice piece of ass," the man said. "You ripping off some of that?"

Robert Biggers stared at him.

"Look," the man said, "I don't care what you're doing. I was just asking. Now get the hell over there and mind your own goddamned business. Go on."

Robert Biggers returned to his desk.

At eight fifty-two the time lock released. Harry Burrell and the other two men emerged from Burrell's office. One man stood with a revolver pointed at Mr. Burrell. The other two men stuck their guns in their belts and removed green plastic bags from under their coats. They entered the vault. In a while one of them emerged with two bags bulging. He went inside again. In a few minutes, both of the men came out.

"May I have your attention?" Mr. Burrell said. "I am going to leave now with these men. We are going to my house. We will pick up the man who is still at my house. Then I will go with these men. They will release me when they feel they are safe. For my sake, do nothing until ten o'clock. Keep the shades drawn until nine-fifteen. Then let people in, and do the best you can to appear calm and that everything is all right. If anyone wants a large sum in currency, tell them the time lock is stuck and I've gone to get assistance. Is that clear?"

The tellers nodded.

Mr. Burrell and the man with him left by the rear door. The other two men stood at the vault. They had their guns out again. One of them put his gun in his belt. The other held his gun in his right hand. Each man stooped slightly to pick up the green plastic bags.

Robert Biggers moved his left foot slowly to the left under the desk and hit the alarm button. His face relaxed as he hit it. It was a silent alarm. It rang only in the police station.

The man with the gun in his hand said: "What did you do?"

Robert Biggers looked at him.

"I said what did you do?" the man said.

Robert Biggers stared at him.

"You hit the fucking alarm," the man said. "You stupid fuck."

"I didn't," Robert Biggers said.

"You lying bastard," the man said. The black revolver came up slowly. "I told you not to do that. And you did it. You stupid fuck."

The revolver kicked hard against the man's bent right arm. As it kicked, Biggers was coming out of the chair to protest. The slug caught him in the belly and he reeled backward in the chair. The second slug hit him just to the right of the center of his chest and tipped him over the right arm of his chair, the surprised, innocent, protesting look still on his face.

"The rest of you motherfuckers," the man said, "get in the fucking vault."

The tellers began to scramble. Nancy Williams had a perplexed expression on her face.

"*Get in the fucking vault,*" the man said. He waved them into the vault. He slammed the door behind them and spun the locking wheel. "Come on," he said.

The second man was already halfway down the corridor to the rear entrance, carrying all three bags of money. In the business area of the bank, Robert L. Biggers bled over the arm of the chair, the blood dripping down slowly onto the gold and orange carpeting, the look of stunned, protesting innocence settling into the features of his face.

In the parking lot the two men hurled the bags of oney into a white Plymouth sedan. In a green Pontiac sedan, the first man sat with Harry Burrell. The man who had shot Biggers shouted: "Bingo. For Christ sake, Bingo."

The first man brought his revolver up and whacked Harry Burrell at the base of his skull with the barrel. Burrell sagged off to the left of the rear seat. The man stripped his mask off, opening the door as he did so. "I'll get him," he said. "Same place. Go."

The other two men were backing the Plymouth around. It left the parking lot swiftly, but without peeling any rubber. When it reached the parking lot in front of the bank, it was moving quickly, but not conspicuously so. Each of the occupants had removed his nylon stocking.

The green Pontiac emerged from behind the bank and swung through the parking lot. It proceeded east, in the direction opposite from that taken by the other car.

21

THE RECEPTIONIST spoke apologetically. "I asked him for his name, Mr. Foley," she said, "and he wouldn't give it."

Foley said that was all right and picked up the telephone. "Foley," he said.

"This is Eddie," the voice said. "I know you're busy and all, but I was wondering how that turned out. Did you make the grab?"

"Yeah," Foley said. "I was going to try to get in touch with you and then I decided it'd be better if I didn't. Yeah, it went fine, just fine. He had five M-sixteens, just like you said."

"*Okay,*" Eddie said. "Glad to hear it. He's gonna get indicted and all?"

"I think so," Foley said.

"Fine," Eddie said. "Now does that do it?"

"Do what?" Foley said.

"You said you needed a reason," Eddie said. "That day I saw you, we talked about this New Hampshire thing, and you said you needed a reason. You gonna come up there with me now and tell them what a nice guy I am?"

"You mean that truck thing," Foley said. "The booze."

"Hey, Dave," Eddie said, "don't jerk my chain, okay? You know what I mean. You gonna go through for me?"

"I already made the call," Foley said. "I called the U.S. Attorney up there and I told him you were instrumental in bringing about a major arrest, and that as a result of your cooperation, we confiscated five stolen military machineguns and arrested a known dealer in stolen guns. Okay?"

"I hope so," Eddie said. "You think it'll work?"

"I dunno," Foley said, "he's pretty mean, that guy up there. He took it all down and I asked him what he thought of it, and he said: 'Well, it's a start, anyway.'"

"What does that mean?" Eddie said.

"I told him we couldn't've made the case without you, and he said: 'All right. Now, is he working on anything else for you? I'd like it better if he was working on something else for you.'"

"Anything else?" Eddie said. "He isn't satisfied?"

"I don't know whether he's satisfied or not," Foley said. "I'm telling you what he said. He said he'd like it better if you were working on something else for us. You know how it is, it's one thing to just go and trade one guy for another one, but when you got a guy that's joined up, that's going to be sending you some more stuff, well, you got more to go with, is all. I suppose that's what's on his mind."

"Shit," Eddie said.

"Hey look," Foley said, "I don't blame the guy. He's in a different district, you know? His guys grabbed you and grabbed you fair and square. And you didn't plead out on him, you made him go through a trial and you didn't have a prayer of winning, just because you didn't want to play ball with him."

"He wanted me to fink on the guys that stole the stuff," Eddie said.

"Well, I know that," Foley said. "You can't blame him for that, can you? And you wouldn't tell him. So he convicted you and now he's got you in the box, and somebody from another district calls him up and says: 'Coyle did *me* a favor. Leave him go.' It's only natural the man's going to say, 'Well, that's very nice, but what'd he do for me? I still don't have the guys that stole the booze. Why should I be doing favors for a guy that isn't doing me any favors?' And what do I say to that? I'd feel the same way, I was to get a call from somebody in New Hampshire telling me Jackie Brown did something for him. Dandy. But what's Jackie Brown done for *me?*"

"*Is* the kid doing anything for you?" Eddie said.

"Let me put it this way," Foley said. "I think he's giving it some very serious thought. I kind of dropped it on him he was looking at a five-year stretch, and we might have to turn him over to the State, even though we didn't want to, and if we did, well, if the State catches you with a machinegun, it's life and forever plus two years on and after. He asked me what he'd probably get if he was convicted in federal court, and I leveled with him, I said it depends on the judge, probably anywhere from two years minimum to five years, the full route. Then, by then he's been arraigned and made bail and so forth, and we're in the elevator, and he says, 'Okay, I'll be seeing you, I guess. Where do I get my car back?' And I give him the look and then the bad news: 'You don't get the car back, Jackie,' I said. 'That car was a vehicle being used to commit a crime, to transport contraband. It's forfeited to the United States of America.' And he looks at me like he can't believe it and he says he paid four thousand dollars for the car, and I tell him, 'Look, I know how you feel. But we don't have no choice. That car is gone, and you might

as well get used to it. It'll be put into government service. Kiss the car goodbye.' So he looks at me and I tell
him some more: 'The guy that had that Charger I'm
driving,' I said, 'he felt the same way. It's a tough
thing, but there it is.' So he knows we're not kidding,"
Foley said. "I wouldn't be surprised if he came
around."

"Look," Coyle said, "I can't give him the guys he
wants in New Hampshire. You got to call him up and
explain that to him. If I do that I am dead, is all there is
to it. He can't ask me to go out and commit suicide for
him."

"He's not asking you for anything," Foley said. "He
didn't ask you for Jackie Brown. That was your idea.
You're the one that's asking for something."

"You were the one that said it," Coyle said. "You said
you hadda have a reason. So I give you a reason."

"That's right," Foley said. "I said I wouldn't make
any calls for you unless you did something for me. So
you did something for me, and I went through, I made
the call, just like it was our understanding. But the man
I made the call to, he never got into this. He didn't say
he'd go to the judge if you got us a grab. He didn't
know a goddamned thing about it. I never said he did.
You tipped us on Jackie so I'd make a call for you, and
I made the call. You just don't like what the call got
you. I can't help that, Eddie. You're a big boy now."

"So now I got to do something for him," Coyle said.
"How the fuck do I do that? I'm never up in New
Hampshire, I don't know anything about what's going
on up there."

"You knew about the booze," Foley said. "You knew
and you wouldn't tell. You were a stand-up guy.

Stand-up guys go to jail, in most jurisdictions I know about."

"I couldn't tell him about the booze," Eddie said. "They'd've killed me. He should be able to understand that."

"He probably does understand it," Foley said. "And anyway, he isn't saying—he didn't say you had to tell him about the booze. He said he'd like it better if he could go in to the judge and say you were a guy that made one good case for the uncle and was working on some others. Then he'd feel better about it, because it'd show that you rehabilitated yourself, that you weren't just giving us a ransom for some time in jail for you. What he wants is something like that, is what I think."

"You're telling me I gotta turn stoolie permanent," Eddie said. "Permanent goddamned fink."

"I'm telling you nothing of the kind," Foley said. "You don't have to do anything you don't want to do, except one thing: you got to be in federal district court in New Hampshire in three weeks for disposition of a charge of stolen goods. That you got to do. If you don't, they'll put out a capias on you and the marshals'll pick you up and drag you in. But that's the only thing you got to do. Anything else you do is because you want to."

"It ain't right," Eddie said. "You set me up."

"Look, Eddie," Foley said, "you go some place and have yourself a glass of beer and a long talk with yourself. The only one fucking Eddie Coyle is Eddie Coyle. You wanted a call. You gave me a grab to get the call. You got the call. You want something else, you start thinking about how to get that. You know where to reach me. You don't want to reach me, that's also all right. No hard feelings. We're fair and square. I can certainly understand a man doesn't want to rat on his friends. I know that. You got to understand the position I'm in. All I can give you is what I tell you I can give you, and I gave you that. What you do next is entirely up to you."

"I should've known better'n to trust a cop," Eddie said. "My goddamned mother could've told me that."

"Everybody oughta listen to his mother," Foley said. "You know where to reach me if you want to talk."

CORPORAL VARDENAIS of the Massachusetts State Police was eating breakfast at two o'clock in the morning at the Eastern Airlines lunchroom at Logan Airport. Propped before him was the *Record*. He was reading a story headlined: "2ND BANKER DIES OF WOUNDS IN W. MARSHFIELD STICKUP." The story said that Branch Manager Harold W. Burrell had died of a skull fracture suffered three days before when he was pistol-whipped during a sixty-eight thousand dollar robbery. It mentioned the shooting to death of Robert L. Biggers.

Wanda Emmett, wearing her Northeast uniform, took the counter seat next to Corporal Vardenais. "You say hello to your friends since you got promoted, Roge?" she said.

"Hey, Wanda," Corporal Vardenais said, "how you hitting them?"

"Not bad," she said. "Not good. You know."

"You coming or going?" Vardenais said.

"I just got in," she said. "I got the Miami run now. Out yesterday, back today."

"Good trip?" he said.

"You know," she said, "not much business this time of year. I kind of like it this way, but then I start thinking how it'll be in a month or so, whole plane filled, screaming kids, women always wanting something. I get just as down thinking about it as I do when it actually happens. Funny, huh?"

"What're you doing over here?" Vardenais said.

"I left my car here," she said. "I was late getting here

when I went out and the lot was full. So I left it here."

"I wouldn't think you'd drive," Vardenais said. "Ought to be simpler to take a cab over, I should think."

"Oh," she said, "I don't live over Beacon Street any more. I moved out."

"How come?" he said.

"Well," she said, "I got a better offer. At least I thought it was a better offer at the time. I was sick of Susie and her goddamned curlers, and then I heard about this other thing, so I moved out."

"Where you living now?" he said.

"You aren't gonna believe this," she said. "Up in Orange. I live up in Orange."

"God," Vardenais said, "that's way up and hell and gone. How far is that, about a three hour drive?"

"Couple hours," she said. "I was thinking, it'd be good for skiing and all. It wasn't a very good idea."

"You got an apartment up there?" he said.

"Trailer," she said. "I live in a trailer."

"How are them things?" he said. "I was thinking, I got my tax bill last week, and I was thinking maybe I should look into one of those things. Are they all right?"

"You couldn't do it," she said. "You got, how many, two kids? It'd drive your wife nuts. I mean, there's only two of us, and sometimes I'm not there, and still, it's awful cramped and all. I don't think you could do it. There isn't any place to put anything, you know? And you can't get any privacy at all. You wouldn't like it."

"I guess not," Vardenais said. "Jesus, though, it just about breaks your heart when you get that tax bill. I start thinking, it's costing me about two, three dollars a day just to live in that town."

"Hey Roge," Wanda said, "we're still friends now, aren't we?"

"Sure," he said.

"Well," she said, "why I ask, if I was to tell you something, as a friend and all, could you sort of keep my name out of it, you know?"

"Sure," he said. "I could at least try, anyway."

"Uh, uh," she said. "Trying's not good enough. You got to really keep my name out of it. Otherwise I'm not gonna tell you."

"Okay," he said, "your name's out of it."

Wanda opened her handbag and removed a light green bankbook. On the cover it said: "First Florida Federal Savings and Loan."

"See this?" she said.

"Yeah," he said.

"I just made a deposit yesterday," she said. "Opened the account. Five hundred dollars."

"Yeah," he said.

Wanda opened the handbag again. She produced a packet of red, blue, tan, and green bankbooks, held together with a thick rubber band. "Same with these," she said. "I made deposits in all of these yesterday too."

"All Florida banks," he said.

"All Florida," she said. "Two weeks ago I took a comp trip, I went over to Nassau. I opened some bank accounts there, too. And I got some more bankbooks up in Orange, too."

"How many've you got, all together?" Vardenais said.

"I think it's about thirty-five, now," she said. "About thirty-five, maybe forty."

"How much in them," she said.

"Well," she said, "offhand I would say about forty-five thousand dollars. More or less, something like that."

"That's a lot of money for a working girl to have," Vardenais said.

"It sure is," she said. "And the funny thing is, it was all in cash. Nothing bigger'n fifties."

"I think I'm in the wrong line of work," Vardenais said. "The last time I saw a bankbook with my name on it, it said something about a mortgage. I didn't know there was anybody who actually had money to put away for himself. I thought money was for paying for things."

"I didn't say my name was on any of these," she said.

"Whose name is?" he said. "You think I'd recognize it if I was to hear it?"

"There's more'n one name," she said. "I don't think you'd recognize any of them. See, I know the guy who made them up, and I don't think any of them are really real people, you know? I think they're all just him."

"He must be a very wealthy guy," Vardenais said.

"He hid it pretty well, if he was," she said. "I sure didn't know anything about it, if he was."

"He have a rich uncle die and leave him some money?" Vardenais said.

"Three rich uncles," she said, "and all of them died this month or so."

"Isn't that funny?" Vardenais said.

"Isn't it," she said. "I understand there's another one that's in pretty poor health, too."

"Were they all in the banking business?" Vardenais said.

"He doesn't tell me much about them," she said. "The only way I know is, he gets up very early in the morning and leaves, and then he comes back in the afternoon, maybe, and he's very excited. He'll drink, say, eight or nine scotches and he's very interested in the papers that day, and watching television. Around suppertime he's always got a headache, so he can't drive, and I have to go out and get the papers. Oh yeah, and he's got one of them big, eight-band radios, that get, you know, AM and FM and short wave and airplanes, and what's the other one, police calls. That's it, police calls. When he goes out to visit one of his uncles he takes that radio with him in the car, and when he comes back, he brings the radio inside, and he listens to that all night, too. But anyway, that's when I know one of his uncles isn't feeling well, and he's been out visiting him."

"Does anybody else go with him?" Vardenais said.

"Not that I know about," she said. "Sometimes there's a man comes to see him, and they talk, and the man leaves a paper bag that's awful heavy, like it had something made of metal in it. That happened once. It was just before one of the uncles died, too. He also gets very tense when he thinks one of his uncles is getting sick. There isn't any phone in the trailer, you know? And when he thinks one of his uncles is getting sick, he's always going out for a little while, to make some calls."

"Checking on the health," Vardenais said.

"I suppose so," she said. "Then, a few days or so later, he gives me these envelopes, ordinary white envelopes, and he tells me to take them and he gives me this list of names that I think he made up, and I have to spend my whole layover running around down there in Florida, opening bank accounts."

"How long do you think it'll be before the one that's sick now passes away?" Vardenais said.

"That's hard to say," she said. "One just died, the day before yesterday, and it's funny, but they usually don't die right together. It seems like they die about a week or so apart, and they always get sick, like I said, very early in the morning, he has to go and see them. I wouldn't be surprised if the one that's still alive made it into next week. But if I was that uncle, I think I wouldn't make any plans beyond, say, Tuesday morning."

"You wouldn't have any idea where the one that's still alive lives, would you?" Vardenais said.

"I tell you," she said. "I was home the other day and this guy he calls Arthur came up, but I was in the bathroom at the time and so he answered the door himself, which he doesn't generally do. I guess he figures, I'm a stew, I ought to stay in condition for waiting on people hand and foot. Anyway, he was in a real mean mood. He was all lathered up about something, I could tell because he was forgetting how nice I been to him, and how I used up all my layovers running around doing his banking for him, and he clipped me a couple times because I guess I said something he didn't like. So I was in the bathroom fixing my hair, and he lets this Arthur in, and I couldn't hear everything they were saying, but Arthur was all upset too. So they're talking, and this and that, and very low voices, and Arthur says, 'Well, what does this do to Lynn?' And my friend there says, 'Well, it isn't going to do anything to Lynn, is all,' and what they have to do, all they have to do, is make damned sure Fritzie doesn't go off half-cocked again, is all. They just take him to Whelan's and leave Donnie at the bank this time, because nobody's figured anything out yet and they can finish what they started. Then he says, my friend says: 'And keep your goddamned voice down, will you? She's in there. You know you can't trust no woman.' "

"So you think this other uncle lives in Lynn," Vardenais said. "You got any idea where in Lynn?"

"I really don't," she said. "That's all I heard, what I told you."

"You think maybe you could find out where in Lynn, and give me a call?" Vardenais said.

"No," she said, "I really don't. Like I said, they don't say very much in front of me, except my friend likes to talk about fucking me in front of his friends, he does that, it's okay to talk about that. But otherwise they generally include me out of things, you know?"

"Yeah," Vardenais said. "Well, I appreciate this, Wanda."

"That's all right," she said. "Hey, my name's out of it, all right? No maybes, now, because I could get hurt."

"Yeah," Vardenais said. "Hey, this is Jimmy we're talking about, that's got all the uncles, right?"

"I can't think of his name right this minute," she said. "It'll probably come to me, though."

"Thanks, Wanda," Vardenais said.

"It's all right, Roge," she said. "You always been a pretty nice guy."

23

DILLON SAID he wasn't sure that Foley would be interested in what he had. "I thought about it some," he said, "I don't like to drag a man out for something that probably isn't so important, I mean, you got things to do and all. Then I think, well, let him decide for himself, if it's not important, okay, but it might be, you know? So I appreciate you coming out."

They stood in front of the Waldorf and faced the Public Garden. On the other side of the intersection of Arlington and Boylston Streets there was an organ grinder with a sign that asked for business at parties and social occasions. Well-dressed people avoided him as they emerged from Shreve's; one plump man in a tweed jacket stood in the chill gray air with a fatuous smile on his face.

"You want to go inside for some coffee?" Foley said.

"I don't think so," Dillon said. "I been having some trouble with my stomach, and I think probably it's all the coffee I been drinking. I keep a pot there behind the bar, you know, so while I'm selling the booze to the people, I'm swigging that stuff all the time. I generally put away about two and a half pots in a day, and I guess probably that's too much. I feel like I wanta throw up, you know?"

Across the street from the organ grinder several boys and girls with extremely long hair stood around in Army parkas. A few sat on the steps of the Arlington Street Church. On each side of Arlington Street there was a tall young man selling papers.

"We could have some tea," Foley said.

"No thanks," Dillon said. "I hate tea. My old lady, when I was married, there, she was always throwing down the tea. I can't stand the stuff. If I was to drink something it'd be coffee, you know. I'll drink a glass of buttermilk when I get somewhere, and that'll make it feel better."

The tall young man on the Public Garden side of Arlington Street stepped off the curb each time the traffic lights halted a group of cars. He walked between the lanes, waving his papers and bending to look into car windows.

"Now what the fuck is he selling?" Dillon asked. "Is that the thing that got banned, there?"

"It's probably *The Phoenix*," Foley said. "I come through there the other night and it was *The Phoenix* then."

"What's that?" Dillon said. "Is that the one they got arrested for selling, there?"

"I don't think so," Foley said. "I think that was another one, I forget the name of it. I dunno what that thing is. I didn't buy one."

"Probably sells maybe two a day," Dillon said. "What the hell's he trying to prove, anyway?"

"Look," Foley said, "it's something to do."

"Yeah," Dillon said. "Something to do. Crazy bastards, they could go out and work, you know, they want something to do. I had a guy come in the other night, he had this thing, *Screw*, that's the name of it. You know what they got in that?"

"Dirty pictures," Foley said.

"*Every*thing," Dillon said. "Christ, they had this one picture there, apparently the guy sent it in himself.

There he is inna park in the snow, stark staring bare-ass naked, and his big cock hanging down there. Got a big grin on his face. Figure that one out."

"He was probably hot," Foley said.

"Yeah," Dillon said, "that's probably it. This friend of mine, he's got one of them bookstores down there, you know? Sells, I figure he sells beaver pictures. And he does. He tells me, though, he does a pretty good business in pictures of boys, too, boys with big dicks. I ask him, who buys them, and he says, the same guys that buy the other stuff, the ones of the girls."

"It's a funny world," Foley said.

"The longer I'm in it the funnier it gets," Dillon said. "I wouldn't think they could bring that kind of stuff inna the country, you know? Why the hell don't you guys stop chasing around bothering people that're minding their own business there, and stop some of that crap that's coming in?"

"Hey," Foley said, "you're not getting me on the pussy posse. That's Post Office, or Customs or something. I don't want nothing to do with that shit. Besides, that'd put your friend out of business. You wouldn't want to do that?"

"Dave," Dillon said, "I got a strong notion you couldn't put my friend outa business with anything short of a bomb, you know? I know this guy about six years now, I never see him take a bust, I never see him in any kind of trouble, he's always got a few dollars on him, dresses fucking respectable, always got a shirt and tie on, and I think this is probably about the ninth thing he's been doing. He hadda bar for a while, then he was doing something in show business, I see him last year at the track, he's got a nice Cadillac. Last year he invited me to go down to New Orleans, there, to the Super Bowl, and he picks up the whole tab for me, plane fare, ticket, everything, and I say to him, what do you want from me, and you know what he says? He says: 'I thought you'd like to see the game, is all.' And it really was. A genuine nice guy."

"What's he doing selling beaver pictures, then?" Foley said.

"Well," Dillon said, "that's what I mean. I asked him and he said: 'Hey, people want to buy the stuff. You think I care what turns a guy on? That's his business. He wants to buy something, who the hell am I to say he can't? Huh? I happen to like something else, that's my business, I never see one of the people that buy these things coming around and saying I can't do what I like, so where's the problem?' I ask him, I say, don't you think, maybe the guys that buy these things go around getting little kids, and he says: 'No, I think they go home and beat the hog over them, is what I think.' So how do you know, a thing like that? I can't figure it out."

"Hey, look," Foley said, "what *is* going on, anyway?"

"Oh," Dillon said, "yeah. Well, I don't know as I really know, you know? But there was this thing, well, you remember we were talking about Eddie Fingers, there, last time I see you?"

"He was getting a lot of telephone calls," Foley said.

"Yeah," Dillon said. "From Jimmy Scal."

"And he was all upset," Foley said.

"*All* upset," Dillon said. "Beating the hell out of the sauce and everything."

"Yeah," Foley said.

"Well, I see now where he's got a lot of money," Dillon said. "That's unusual for him. He goes along all right usually, seems to have a couple of dollars on him, but he's got a lot of money now."

"Like how much?" Foley said.

"Well, I couldn't tell you, exactly," Dillon said. "I just had a glimpse of the roll, you know? But there was some fair-sized bills in there, and I would have to say, probably he's got a couple of thousand dollars there, at least."

"How'd you happen to see it?" Foley said.

"He was in the other night," Dillon said. "He orders up a shot and a beer, comes in about seven, seven-thirty or so, which is another thing that's unusual for him, you know? Either he comes in in the afternoon or else you won't see him until probably pretty late. But he comes in right after supper the other day and orders up, and I serve him, and he sits there, reading the Seven Races and so on, doesn't want to make any conversation, and then this other guy comes in, a little time goes by and this other guy comes in."

"You know the other guy?" Foley said.

"Well, let's say I know him, I'd recognize him if I was to see him again, all right? But I don't happen to remember his name right now, if it's all the same to you. I'd rather leave him out of this if I can."

"Okay," Foley said.

"So this other guy comes in and him and Eddie, Eddie gets up from the bar and they go sit inna booth, you know? So they're talking there, and I see the other guy doesn't have anything in front of him and his cred-it's all right, so I make up a little bourbon on the rocks, Wild Turkey, and a Budweiser, and I go over there and put it in front of this other fellow. And Eddie's got this big wad of money there that he's putting into his pocket, and the other guy's picking up a few bills from the table. So that's when I see it."

"You wouldn't have any idea what they might have been doing," Foley said.

"Hey," Dillon said, "I'm serious, now, the other guy stays out of it."

"Okay," Foley said, "I'm not after him, I was just asking."

"Well, it's got nothing to do with what we were talking about, is all," Dillon said. "Look, between you and me, I wouldn't be surprised if Eddie was maybe buying a television set, you know? A color tee-vee? But that is strictly between us. I'm not throwing nobody else in. The money means something you know about, all right. But the other guy is not included in this."

"Okay," Foley said. "What do you make of the money?"

"I don't know," Dillon said. "Like I say, Eddie's not the kind of guy that you expect to see with a lot of dough, you know? So I see it, and then I think, well, I wonder if maybe this is something you oughta know about and all. Has he got any beef with you?"

"Let me put it this way," Foley said. "He's got a beef with the United States, but that's up in New Hampshire, for when he was trucking booze there. So maybe that's a beef with me, I don't know."

"I thought that was all over," Dillon said. "I thought he took the fall on that, back there, back in when was it — last month or something? A while ago, anyway."

"He got convicted," Foley said, "but he's coming up

for sentencing next month there, I understand. There was some kind of new trial hassle, or something. Maybe it's sooner, I don't know."

"What could he get for that?" Dillon said. "That mean jail?"

"I don't really know very much about the case," Foley said. "We don't enforce in that area, you know? I suppose there's a possibility of some jail. I really don't know. I just happen to hear somebody mention the case the other day, and that's why I was thinking about it when you said that, you know?"

"Eddie don't like jail," Dillon said.

"Well," Foley said, "very few guys do. I know quite a few that went to jail at one time or another and there wasn't more'n one or two of them that you could really say, that actually liked it, you know?"

"Yeah," Dillon said, "but look, he must *know*. I mean, he's talked to somebody about it, hasn't he? He's got some idea."

"I suppose so," Foley said.

"Well," Dillon said, "now I wonder what the fuck he's buying a color tee-vee for when he's probably going to jail in a little while."

"Maybe a little present for the wife," Foley said, "keep her happy and home while he's doing time."

"I kind of doubt it," Dillon said. "I know Eddie more or less and that isn't something he'd do. He don't get along that good with her."

"He got a girlfriend?" Foley said. "Maybe it's a little present for the girlfriend."

"Nope," Dillon said, "he takes a little off now and then, but no girlfriend. I don't think he thinks about it that much, getting laid. They letting you bring a tee-vee to jail with you now?"

"They weren't," Foley said, "not the last I heard."

"I don't think so," Dillon said, "I didn't remember anything like that from before when I was in, either. No, I think Eddie thinks probably he isn't gonna go to jail there, and I wonder why he thinks that."

"I wonder where he got the money," Foley said. "That's what bothers me. I always understood he was just getting by. I wonder what he's been doing to get all that money."

"It's kind of interesting, isn't it?" Dillon said. "I tell you what, you go and think about how come a little fish has got a lot of money all of a sudden, and I'll go and think about how come a man that's got the kind of record he's got doesn't think he'll go to jail on that booze thing, and maybe I'll talk to some people and get back to you, all right?"

"Fine," Foley said. "I'll expect to hear from you."

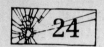 **24**

It was getting light along the shore drive in Nahant at quarter of six on Tuesday morning when Fritzie Webber parked the blue Le Sabre. Scalisi came up behind him in a tan Chevrolet sedan; Arthur Valantropo sat in the back seat of the Chevrolet. It laid down a thin blanket of condensed exhaust in the cold air of early morning, while Webber locked the Buick and got into the Chevrolet.

"Okay?" Scalisi said. He was wearing a green nylon windbreaker and he had a nylon stocking pulled over his head. In the back, Arthur Valantropo was rolling the fabric of another stocking over his features, compressing them slowly into something strange. Webber removed a stocking from his jacket pocket. He nodded.

"No tails or anything?" Valantropo said.

"Nothing I could see," Webber said, "all the way from Fall River I was alone on the road. If they're watching me, they're doing it from an airplane. How about Donnie, he okay?"

"We saw him turn off back there," Scalisi said, taking the Chevrolet into the street. "He give us the thumbs-up, so I guess it's all right."

"Good," Webber said, the mask now covering his face. "I wonder what the fuck it was got Dillon so stirred up then?" He reached under the seat and pulled out a paper bag. He took a Python three-fifty-seven magnum revolver from it and released the cylinder lock. From his jacket pocket he brought five bullets and began loading them into the chambers.

"He was worried about Coyle," Scalisi said. "I believe him. He was wondering if maybe Coyle was swapping us for that thing he's got going up in New Hampshire, there."

"He still could be," Valantropo said.

The Chevrolet moved off the shore drive into a residential street. Large houses, built around the turn of the century, sat well back from the road behind low stone walls and hedges still green in the late autumn.

"No way," Scalisi said. "He didn't know anything. I never told him a goddamned thing. All he knew was we wanted some guns. Far as he knows, we're using them for target practice."

"That was before we did anything," Valentropo said. "Soon's we pulled the first one, he knew. Coyle's not stupid, you know."

"I know he's not," Scalisi said. "I also know he's got a funny hand from being careless. He's too smart to get careless 'long that line again. And besides, what if he is trying to throw us in, what if he did want to dump us? What could he tell them? He could tell them what we did, maybe, what he thinks we been doing. But he doesn't know where we're going to be either, not until we been there. I tell, I tell you, there's just no way Coyle could set us up."

Scalisi steered the Chevrolet into the long curved driveway at 16 Pelican Hill. The tires made a crunching sound on the white stones. Some one hundred yards in from the street, a rambling gray and white, gabled three-story house stood comfortably in the wind from the sea.

"This Whelan character's doing all right for himself," Webber said. "He got any kids we know about?"

"Grown up and moved away," Valantropo said. "Just him and his wife. She's a nice lady. She'll probably fix you up some hot breakfast while you're waiting for us."

"I don't like this waiting stuff," Webber said. "I'm glad this is the last one. I get nervous sitting around like this, not knowing what's going on."

"You got nervous being in the bank, too," Valantropo said. "Which is why Donnie's there and you're here this time, instead of the other way."

"Hey, look," Webber said, "I wasn't the only one. Jimmy hit that old guy a pretty good whack too, from what I see inna papers anyway."

"He must've had a thin skull," Scalisi said. "I hit a few guys in my time a lot harder'n that, without killing them."

"Yeah," Valantropo said, "and let's just remember Jimmy hadda hit that guy because you blew it already in the bank. I told you and told you, killing somebody's the surest way in the world to get a goddamned army out after you."

"Look," Webber said, "he pulled the fucking alarm. Didn't he pull the alarm? We told them, we said: 'Lay off the alarm or you're gonna get hurt.' We told them that. For Christ sake. I say, they don't do what you tell them they should do, you gotta do it. I don't care, I say you gotta hit them."

"Not when you already got the money," Valantropo said. "It happens when you just go in, I agree with you. You got to protect yourself. Of course. But when you're going out, when you got the money, no. When you're halfway out the door, for Christ sake, I mean, where's the percentage in that? What does it get you, shooting when you're going out and they pull the alarm, huh? Does it stop the alarm? You think maybe the alarm doesn't go off if you shoot the guy that pulled it? No, it just makes things worse, is all. You don't get any more time to get away in. You just get everybody all pissed off and they start running around and everything. It don't pay, it just don't pay at all. And I say, I say you don't shoot somebody unless it's gonna help you."

"Yeah," Webber said. "Well, I don't agree with you."

The Chevrolet moved slowly up the driveway and came to a quiet stop at the garage. Scalisi turned off the ignition very slowly, as though that would lessen the change in the noise level.

"Okay," Valantropo said, "you don't agree with me. Fuck you and do like I say."

"Both of you bastards shut up and let's go to work," Scalisi said in a hushed voice. "I'm sick of listening to you."

They got out of the car very slowly and carefully closed each door to the first lock of the latch. In the morning light they looked first at each other through the nylon stockings. Then each of them surveyed the area. They stepped gingerly on the crushed stone of the driveway, and from there to the lawn. They approached the house in single file, walking in the grass at the edge of the crushed stone walk, the white frost melting and wetting their sneakers. Close to the back door of the house, Scalisi and Valantropo hung back six or seven paces behind Webber. Each of them had his revolver in his hand. Webber shifted his revolver to his left hand. Holding the gun toward the sky, Webber removed from his sleeve a thin metal spatula with a wooden handle. He moved from the grass onto the first of the steps leading to the back door. Scalisi and Valantropo positioned themselves at angles to the steps.

Webber crouched at the screen door and peered at the area around the knob. Placing the spatula in his teeth, he worked the handle of the door. It opened slowly, with no sound. Behind the screen door there was a wooden door with nine small panes of glass set into it. Scalisi, holding the screen door now with his left hand, bent forward behind Webber to stare at the jamb near the knob.

"How's it look?" Scalisi said, whispering.

"Standard cylinder," Webber said, also whispering. He straightened up briefly and peered in through the glass.

"Chain lock?" Scalisi whispered.

"No," Webber whispered. His left hand came back and stuck the Python in his belt at the hip. He bent forward again. Scalisi could see the blade of the spatula passing between the edge of the door and the jamb. Scalisi heard a metallic sound. He saw Webber exert some pressure against the door. The door swung silently open.

Valantropo was on the steps now. Leaving wet footprints, they went into the back entry. In the gentle light of morning, they brushed past coats on hooks inside the entryway, then climbed three worn stair treads and opened another door into the kitchen. Except for the soft squeegee sound of their wet sneakers on the floor, the house was silent.

Webber turned around in the kitchen and tried to smile behind the nylon mask. "Okay?" he whispered.

In the yard behind the house and garage, Ernie Sauter rested the butt of the Winchester twelve-gauge on his hip and waved toward the bushes behind the house. Deke Ferris, bent over, ran toward the garage. He carried a Thompson submachinegun. Sauter looked toward the second story of the house. At the edge of the window overlooking the back door, Sauter saw Tommy Damon. Sauter raised his hand, palm upward. Damon's face disappeared from the window.

In the kitchen, Scalisi padded cautiously toward the door at the other end. It had a glass plate at waist level on the frame. He put his gloved hand on the plate and pushed. The door swung away silently. Scalisi looked into the hall. He let the door come back slowly. He turned to face Valantropo and Webber. He held his thumb up.

Valantropo was near the kitchen table. When Scalisi signaled, Valantropo pulled one of the chairs up and put it quietly down again. He put his revolver on the table. He sat down.

Scalisi came back to the table. He picked up a chair quietly and sat down. He rested his forearms on his thighs, the revolver held loosely in his right hand.

Webber eased his body past Valantropo. He put his revolver on the table. He lifted a chair silently and sat down. He whispered: "What's the timing?"

Scalisi said: "The old guy gets up first and comes down here, from what I could see. I don't know when the old lady comes down. We got to wait and see."

On the floor above they heard footsteps. They listened intently. More than one person was walking. "Beautiful," Webber said, "Mummy and Daddy coming down together." They listened to the steps on the stairs. They picked up their revolvers. They were all facing the door to the hall when Ferris and Sauter came into the kitchen from the back entryway. As they turned toward the sound, Damon and Rufus Billings came through the hall door with shotguns pointed directly at them. Sauter said: "April fool, motherfuckers." For what seemed like a long time no one moved, and then the three men in masks put their guns carefully on the table.

25

EDDIE COYLE had overslept. When he awoke it was nearly nine. He hurried through his shower and shave. He went into the hall and out into his kitchen in an ugly mood. His wife was watching television and drinking coffee. "Why the hell didn't you wake me up?" he said.

She did not take her eyes off the screen. "Look," she said. "Yesterday I got you up and you give me hell for not letting you sleep. Today I let you sleep and I get hell for not waking you up. What's the matter, you wanta get an early start on the day's loafing?"

"I got things to do today," he said. He poured some coffee. "Look, I got to make some calls."

His wife sighed. She began slowly to get up from the couch. "I know, I know," she said, "go upstairs while I make some calls. Sometimes I think I must be married to the President or something. What's so secret I can't hear what you're saying? I thought I was married to you."

Eddie Coyle said nothing while his wife left the kitchen. In a while he could hear the shower running. He picked up the telephone.

"This is Eddie," he said, when Foley came on the line. "Look, I gotta talk to you."

"So talk," Foley said. "I'm listening."

"You gotta do something," Coyle said. "I want you to do something for me, all right?"

"First I want to hear what it is," Foley said. "Then I

want to know why. You got this problem remembering what's in the deal and what isn't, I seem to recall."

"Look," Coyle said, "never mind that shit. I want you to call New Hampshire and ask him, would it be enough if I was to give you the guys that're robbing the banks, there?"

"What guys," Foley said, "what banks?"

"You know what guys and you know what banks," Coyle said. "I'm not saying I'm gonna do it, now, you understand. I just wanta know, would that do it if I did?"

"Suppose it will," Foley said. "Are you gonna do it?"

'I dunno," Coyle said. He held up his left hand and studied it. "I can think of safer things to do. I dunno. I just want to know, what happens if I decide to, does that get me off the hook."

"Look," Foley said, "I'll ask him. That's all I can do."

"All right," Coyle said. "Can you talk to him by noon?"

"I think so," Foley said. "I should have something for you by then, yeah."

"Okay," Coyle said. "Now, where can I meet you?"

"Whyn't you call me?" Foley said. "I'll be right here."

"No," Coyle said. "I wanta see you, make sure I know everything that's going on."

"Okay," Foley said. "You know over in Cambridge there, in Central Square? You know that area at all?"

"I should," Coyle said, "I grew up there."

"Okay," Foley said. "There's a Rexall there, right at the big intersection. You know the place I mean?"

"Yeah," Coyle said.

"I'll be in that drugstore at noon," Foley said.

"I may not be there," Coyle said.

"I'll be there until twelve-thirty," Foley said. "I can't wait any longer'n that, I got to see a man this afternoon."

"That's okay," Coyle said. "If I'm gonna be there, I'll be there by then. If I'm not, you can assume I decided no."

26

DILLON FOUND the silver Continental with the black vinyl roof in the parking lot at Columbia Station in Dorchester. There was a man in the driver's seat. Dillon opened the passenger's door and got in.

"Sorry to get you up," the man said. He was overweight. He wore sun glasses. He had olive skin and he wore a dark blue suit. He was smoking a cigarette.

"No problem," Dillon said. "I work nights, you know? I don't generally get up until around noon."

"This is kind of an emergency," the man said. "I was wondering if you might be able to handle something for us."

"More'n likely," Dillon said. "Depends, I suppose. But more'n likely."

"This is pretty important," the man said. "That's why I got in touch with you. He told me, he told me I was to get somebody we were sure of, that we could really trust, you know? The kid was pretty close to him, is why we're moving so fast."

"You're getting ahead of me," Dillon said. "Who's the kid?"

"Donnie Goodweather," the man said. "You gotta know him. The man treated him like he was his son. Which some people say he was."

"I never heard of him," Dillon said.

"Well, you're gonna." the man said. "They got him this morning up in Lynn, there."

"Who did?" Dillon said. "Hey, I hate to sound stupid,

and you know me, the man wants it done, I'm here to do it."

"I'm glad to hear that," the man said. "There was some talk around, maybe you were thinking about some grand jury thing or something. I'm really glad to hear you say that. The man'll be pleased, too."

"So what the hell is going on," Dillon said.

"State police," the man said. "Seems Donnie was sitting outside the Colony Cooperative this morning like he was waiting for somebody, and instead of the people he was expecting to show up, some cops with masks and jackets on show up, and he gets out of his car, he's got a mask on too, and a gun, and they tell him he's under arrest, I suppose, and the next thing you know, there's some shooting. He was dead on arrival. The man's very upset."

"Somebody else have a problem?" Dillon said.

"Jimmy Scal and Artie Valantropo and Fritzie Webber," the man said. "They all got bagged in a house up in Nahant this morning. Belongs to this guy that's the treasurer of the Colony Cooperative from what I hear. Jimmy and Artie and the kid went in, and Donnie's waiting down at the bank. So the three of them go in, and the place's crawling with cops. Then the cops take the jackets off Artie Van and Jimmy and the masks, and they go down to the bank with this other cop in the car with them, looking scared, I guess, and they get down there. The cops get out of their car, and with the masks on, of course, you know it's hard to tell, and Donnie gets out of his car, the way I hear it, I was getting all this from Paulie LeDuc, who is Scal's lawyer, he called right up as soon as he talked to Jimmy

up there. So anyway, Donnie gets out of the car and
the cops say: 'Get'em up, you're under arrest.' Well,
he's just a kid, and he always hadda pair of rocks on
him, the man, I think if he wasn't the man's son the
way they say, it's probably because of his guts the man
liked him, and the kid starts shooting. They chewed
him up pretty good."

"Oh oh," Dillon said.

"Oh oh is right," the man said. "The three of them're
up on murder one, they're gonna be having a hearing
this afternoon, and of course they're gonna get held for
the grand jury. The man is hopping goddamned mad."

"I don't blame him," Dillon said.

"Well, I don't blame him either," the man said.

"I blame Jimmy Scal, though," Dillon said. "It's his
own goddamned fault as far as I'm concerned."

"How you figure?" the man said.

"I warned him," Dillon said. "Picked up something
the other day, this guy we both know, me and the Scal,
he's coming up for sentencing pretty soon, and it's almost a mandatory, you know? But this guy don't act
like he thinks he's gonna go to jail, which makes me
very nervous, you know? Why's he so confident, maybe
he's thinking about dumping somebody? So I called
Jimmy, I told him. I said: 'You better hang back a few
days, you got anything going. I don't like the way this
thing smells.' But he wouldn't listen, oh no. Just goes
right ahead."

"This guy," the man said, "anybody we know?"

"Could be," Dillon said. "We hadda break him up a
while back here. He set up Billy Wallace there with a
gun that had a history. We hadda teach him. I thought

he learned his lesson. I threw a little work his way my-self now and then."

"Name of Coyle?" the man said.

"That's the one," Dillon said. "I had him driving a truck for me and a fellow up in New Hampshire there and he got hooked with it. Which was why he was coming up. He didn't talk then, but he had a fall coming and he knew it. I thought maybe he was thinking about dumping me, but of course he wouldn't do that without making a will first. So I guess he dumped Jimmy and Artie instead. Bastard."

"He's the one the Scal mentioned," the man said. "LeDuc give his name to the man. Coyle. Eddie Fingers. That's the one."

"You want him hit?" Dillon said.

"The man wants him hit," the man said. "There's more to it than that. He wants it done tonight."

"I can't do it tonight," Dillon said. "For Christ sake. It takes a little *while*, you know. I got to line some things up, I need a car and a piece and a driver, and I got to set the man up. Christ, I hit a man, I do it right, I don't do it like some goddamned kid that caught his girl fucking somebody else."

"The man says tonight," the man said.

"Well," Dillon said, "you go back and tell him, you say you talked to me and he knows me, he knows who I am, and you tell him: 'Look, Dillon'll make the hit. But he'll make it right, he'll make it so there won't be sixteen hundred squares looking on when he does it.' You tell him that."

"You want to be careful," the man said, "there'll be a contract out on you."

"You betcher ass I want to be careful," Dillon said. "I get a fair price. Five grand in front. Speaking of which, where is it?"

"I haven't got it now," the man said. "You do the job, you get it."

"Oh," Dillon said. "Big fancy Jew-type car, four hundred dollar suit, the shoes, the whole bit, and he wants me to make a hit on the cuff. Lemme tell you something, sweet baby, it don't happen that way. I'm beginning to wonder, did the man send you after all? I never know the man do business like this before. Always very careful, does things inna right way. Not like this, one hand on your dick and the water coming out and the other holding up your goddamned pants when somebody takes your picture. What the fuck's the matter with you guys down there, you blow your cool permanently?"

"Now look," the man said.

"Now look, nothing," Dillon said. "I treat a man with respect, I expect him to treat me with a little respect. He knows how I work, what I do, that's why he wants me. With me it's strictly cash in advance, no money, no hit. I don't accept no credit cards, none at all whatsoever. Now I tell you what, you go and tell the man, you say: 'Dillon's getting it ready, the car, the gun, the whole thing. He'll have it all ready to go the minute you press the button.' Tell him that. And don't come back up here again with no money. I'm willing to do a favor for anybody, but I got to think of some other things too, there's a right way and a wrong way to do everything. Unless maybe you want me to get Coyle arrested or something, I could do that today, and for nothing."

"Don't bush me," the man said. "Don't hand me that crap, you'll get him arrested. The time comes some-body doesn't want to be a man, we'll let you know. You know how to handle these things."

"I do," Dillon said. "That's why I'm having so much trouble understanding what the fuck is going on here. I think there's something funny, maybe. You know where to get in touch with me. I'll line things up, but I don't move until I get the dough, all right?"

"The man isn't going to like it," the man said.

"He came looking for me," Dillon said. "I assume that means he wants me to do something for him, he wants *me*. I had some hard things he asked me to do, and I did them, and nobody got hurt but the guy that was supposed to get hurt. Nobody on anything I ever did ever ended up in the Death House, which is more'n I can say for some I know."

"He knows you're good," the man said.

"All right," Dillon said. "I'll be at the place. You want me, you call me, we'll see what we can do. But we do things the right way, all right?"

"I'll see you," the man said.

27

"HE DIDN'T show up," Foley said. "I sit there for about half an hour, and I have a cheese sandwich and a cup of coffee. Jesus, I forgot how bad a thing a cheese sandwich is to eat. It's just like eating a piece of linoleum, you know?"

"You got to put mayonnaise on it," Waters said. "It's never going to have any flavor at all unless you put some mayonnaise on the bread before you put the cheese on."

"I never heard of that," Foley said. "You put it on the outside, do you?"

"Nah," Waters said, "you put it on the inside. You still put the butter on the outside and all. But when the cheese melts, there, it's the mayonnaise that gives it the flavor. You got to use real mayonnaise, though, the stuff with eggs in it. You can use that other stuff that most people use when they say they're using mayonnaise, that salad dressing stuff, you can use it. But it isn't going to taste the same. I think that other stuff scalds or something. It doesn't taste right, anyway."

"They don't go for those refinements in the Rexall's anyway," Foley said. "What the hell, you go in there and order a cheese sandwich, they got a whole stack of them, already made up, probably since last Wednesday, and they take out one of them goddamned things, big fat piece of this orange cheese in it, and throw on some grease, they pretend it's butter but I sure don't believe that, and then they go and they fuse it all together with a hot press there. My stomach's still trying to break that thing down into something I can live on, just like a big piece, two big pieces, of bathroom tile with some mastic in between. Served hot. I get sick, you're gonna have to give me a pension."

"You been living off the tit too long, I think," Waters said. "Getting so you bastards won't eat anything unless you get it handed up to you at the Playboy Club for God's sake. Undercover. My ass. You think I don't know, you're taking each other to lunch? Shit. Do you good once in a while, the Joe and Nemo route. That's where the hoods are anyway, you know. They don't patronize these high-class joints I'm always seeing on the vouchers, where a piece of meat's nine bucks. They're down scrounging, just like you would be if you couldn't write it up."

"Well anyway," Foley said, "he didn't show. So I'm sitting there and getting the fish-eye from the waitress, and I had a Coke and my bladder's beginning to get sore, you know? So I pay up and get out, and I go out on the street, and I'm not too upset. After all, he said he might not show up. So I part with fifteen cents and I get a *Record*, and what do I see, that the guys he wants to trade off got scooped this morning up in Lynn. So that explains a lot of things."

"One of them got dead," Waters said. "Goodweather, there. I guess he had it in mind to make a fuss or something."

"Yeah," Foley said, "I gotta call Sauter about that. Apologize. I didn't think he was that good a shot. What'd they hit them with?"

"Burglary, for the district court," Waters said. "I imagine the grand jury'll be getting a better variety of charges. Let's see, two murders, three robberies, burglary in all of them bankers' houses, probably gun-running, stolen cars, conspiracy. Did I leave something out?"

"Blasphemy," Foley said. "I always wanted to charge a guy with blasphemy."

"What about your friend with the knuckles, now?" Waters said.

"He goes to jail, looks like," Foley said. "New Hampshire wasn't satisfied he helped us grab Jackie Brown there, and I don't think he's got anything left to trade now."

"Ah, well," Waters said, "tough shit."

28

COYLE CAME into Dillon's place shortly after three-thirty in the afternoon. He took a stool and raised his right hand, then let it fall.

Dillon poured a double shot of Carstairs and drew a stein of draft beer. He put both in front of Coyle. "You making any money?" he said.

Coyle drank off the Carstairs. He drank some of the beer. "I wouldn't exactly put it that way," he said. "Matter of fact, you was to ask me, I'd have to say I'm not having a very good day."

"Hey," Dillon said. "Why is that?"

"You heard what happened up in Lynn there," Coyle said.

"*That* was a rough thing," Dillon said. "I understand that kid there, that got killed, I understand he was in pretty good down in Providence, you know?"

"I didn't hear that," Coyle said. "Gimme some more whiskey." While Dillon was pouring, Coyle talked. "That's about the only thing I didn't hear, though. It figures."

"Well, hell," Dillon said. "It's not as though you had anything to do with it. From what I hear they were all free, white and twenty-one. They knew what they were getting into. They were big boys."

"Yeah," Coyle said. "Course, this is the end of Artie Van. And Jimmy, too, for that matter. On the other hand, how many guys hit the street on murder one, huh? Wouldn't matter they was all virgins. Which they aren't."

"Well," Dillon said, "you got to look at it philosophically, you know? You win some, you lose some. They made, what, about a quarter of a mil in a month? Now you start heaving the pressure on like that, you're gonna get the fuzz mad. It's got to happen. And when that happens, hell, they killed two guys didn't they? When that happens, you take what you get, no money back."

"Yeah," Coyle said, "but they were set up. That's what bothers me, I think. The cops were waiting for them in that house. Somebody set them right fucking up. I'd like to know who that was."

"I imagine they would too," Dillon said. "Yeah, I would think that'd bother them."

"Christ," Coyle said. "I know Jimmy Scal, I know him pretty good. Well, hell, you know that. I known Jimmy since, I known him for a long time. I hate to see him take this one. You know what's going to happen, he's never gonna see the sun shine again. He is in forever."

"You never know," Dillon said. "Maybe they can get the evidence suppressed. That can happen. And a jury'll do funny things, you know. They might get off. You just can't tell about these things."

"They might get off *once*," Coyle said. "They were awful busy, you know. They hit about four counties. I don't think there was one bank they hit was in the same county as another one. Sooner or later somebody's going to take them out. They're all through."

"Well, I still say," Dillon said, "they knew what they were getting into. Did anybody feel sorry for you?"

"No," Coyle said. "You got a lot of fucking nerve asking me that."

"Well," Dillon said, "you went through, didn't you? You took the fall, you didn't come whining to anybody, say, it wasn't my fault, I didn't mean it, look, I'll throw somebody else in, just let me go. You didn't do that. You gotta have as much respect for them as they had for you, you know? You were a big boy, you got to think they're gonna be big boys."

"I haven't been a big boy yet," Coyle said. "That comes up next week."

"I thought it was all over," Dillon said. "I thought that was all wrapped up."

"It is," Coyle said, "I am, I'm all wrapped up. I'm going down to Danbury, is what I'm gonna do."

"How long?" Dillon said.

"My lawyer," Coyle said, "my great goddamned lawyer, he figures about two years, probably."

"So you do eight months," Dillon said, "you do a third. You can do that easy. You'll be out, when, when Gansett opens in the fall. No sweat. And I see you got some money, the other night there. You're all right. Don't take it so goddamned serious."

"I can't help it," Coyle said, "I still feel bad. That Scal, he's a ballsy guy, you know. I dunno Van. But I know the Scal, and he's all right. I feel sorry for the Scal, I really do. He's gonna get life, minimum."

From the other end of the bar a man rose and answered the phone. He shouted: "For you, Dillon."

"I'll be right back," Dillon said. "Get you another on the way?"

"Yeah," Coyle said. "I'll have another beer, too."

Dillon could see Coyle sitting at the bar while he talked on the telephone. "Yeah, I know who this is," he said. "Funny thing, he's in here right now. Putting on a big performance, how sorry he is, how pissed off he is about the way they got set up. Almost enough to make me mad. No, not mad enough for that. Look, you get a man up here this afternoon with the money in an envelope, I'll see what I can do. Maybe tonight, yeah. I'm not promising anything. I still got to get a car. Yeah, I got somebody can drive. The money first. The money in front. Well, you get the money here, I'll see what I can do."

"Look," Dillon said to Coyle, putting the fresh glasses in front of him, "you're gonna step on your tongue, you don't look out. Now, that was a friend of mine, and what he tells me is he can't go to the Broons tonight. So how about you forget your troubles and come to the game with me, huh? We'll have some dinner, I'll take the night off, we see a good game. Rangers. Whaddaya say?"

"Sounds good," Coyle said.

"Sure," Dillon said. "Come back around six or so, I'd say stay but the way you're going, you won't be able to see the game you stay here very much longer. We'll go have a little wine, maybe a steak, then we go to the game. I guarantee you, by the time you get home tonight, you won't have a care inna world."

"I'll do it," Coyle said. "I'll go call my wife."

"Hey, look," Dillon said, "whyn't you forget that for once, all right? You can't tell you know, we might run into something and you wouldn't want to go right home. So, why call her?"

"You're right," Coyle said. "I got some things to do. I'll see you back here around six."

At five-fifteen a kid in a black turtleneck sweater and a suede jacket came into Dillon's place. He asked for

Dillon. He handed Dillon a business envelope, a fairly fat envelope. "Okay?" he said.

"Okay what?" Dillon said.

"Okay?" the kid said. "Just okay."

"If it's okay," Dillon said, "it won't bother you. If it isn't okay, it won't. Get lost."

29

In the course of the evening Coyle had several drinks. He drank beer with Dillon during the first period. Bobby Orr swung the Bruins net and faked three Rangers into sprawls. He quartered across the New York goal, faked low and left, shot high and right, and Coyle rose up with Dillon and fourteen thousand, nine hundred and sixty-five others to howl approval. The announcer said: "Goal to Orr, number four." There was another ovation.

Next to Coyle there was an empty seat. Dillon said: "I can't understand where the fuck he is. That friend of mine, I was telling you about? He give me both his tickets. I invited my wife's nephew. I can't understand where he is. Loves hockey, that kid. I don't know how he stays in school, he's always down here, scrounging for tickets. Twenty years old. But a bright kid."

The kid arrived during the intermission between the first and second periods. He apologized for his tardiness. "I get home," he said, "I get the message all right, but then I have to go and borrow a car. I thought I was gonna miss the goddamned game."

"You couldn't take the trolley or something?" Coyle said.

"Not to fucking Swampscott," the kid said seriously. "You just can't get to Swampscott after nine o'clock. I mean it."

"Hey," Dillon said, "who wants a beer?"

"I'll have a beer," Coyle said. The kid had a beer, too. Dillon had a beer.

In the second period the Rangers opened with a goal on Cheevers. Sanderson went off for roughing. Sanderson came back on. Esposito went off for an elbow check. Sanderson fed Dallas Smith for a shorthanded goal. Orr fed Esposito who fed Bucyk for a goal.

Between the second and third periods, Coyle had trouble following the conversation between Dillon and his wife's nephew. Coyle went to the men's room. As he got up, Dillon observed that he might ask if anybody wanted a beer. Coyle returned with three beers, carried carefully before him. There was beer on his trousers. "Hard to carry beer in a crowd like this," he said.

"You're not supposed to have beer at the seats," the kid said.

"Look," Coyle said, "you want some beer or not?"

During the third period the Rangers got another goal. Sanderson drew a five minute major for fighting. The Bruins won, three to two.

"Beautiful," Coyle said. "Beautiful. Can you imagine being that kid? What is he, about twenty-one? He's the best hockey player inna world. Christ, number four, Bobby Orr. What a future he's got."

"Hey look," Dillon said, "I forgot to tell you. I got some girls."

"Jesus," Coyle said, "I don't know. It's pretty late."

"Come on," Dillon said, "Let's make a night of it."

"Hey," the kid said, "hey, I can't. I gotta get this car back. I got to go home."

"Where's your car?" Dillon said to Coyle.

"Cambridge," Coyle said. "I was over there and I take the trolley in, when I came to your place. I never got back for it."

"Shit," Dillon said. "These girls, I mean, they're absolutely all right. But there isn't any way. I mean, they're in Brookline."

"Well, look," the kid said. "I could drive you to his car, and then go home. I got a test tomorrow, so I can't hang around much."

They had a drink in the tavern on the concourse of the Boston Garden, to let the traffic thin out. Dillon had trouble walking when they got outside. Coyle had more trouble. "You two old bastards," the kid said, "I don't know where you'd be without the youth to help you along." They stumbled over the trolley tracks.

The kid had a 1968 Ford Galaxie, a white sedan. He opened the front passenger door. Dillon and Coyle stood there, weaving back and forth. "Look," Dillon said, "you ride inna front. I'll ride inna back. Okay?"

"Okay," Coyle said. He slid into the passenger seat.

Dillon walked quickly around the back of the car. The kid opened the driver's door, then reached in and unlocked the left rear door.

Dillon got in and sat down behind the driver. Coyle's head lay back on the top of the seat. He was breathing heavily.

"You sure you're gonna be all right to drive," Dillon said.

"Oh yeah," Coyle said, his eyes shut, "Absolutely perfectly all right. No sweat. Beautiful night so far."

"More to come," Dillon said. He reached down to the floor and groped around. On the mat on the right rear passenger side, he found a twenty-two magnum Arminius revolver, fully loaded. He picked it up and put it in his lap.

"I don't know where you want me to go," the kid

said. He was backing the car around over the trolley tracks.

"You tell him," Dillon said to Coyle. Coyle snored.

"Go around the front of the Garden," Dillon said. "Go out past the Registry and head for Monsignor O'Brien Highway, in case he wakes up. You just drive now."

"I know what's going on," the kid said.

"Good," Dillon said, "I'm glad to hear that. You just drive. I was you, I'd drive to Belmont, and I'd pick roads where I could go pretty fast without making anybody suspicious. I'd come out on Route 2, and I'd look for a gray Ford convertible in the parking lot of the West End Bowling Alleys. I wouldn't let nothing disturb me. When I got to the alleys, I'd pull up beside the Ford and get out and get in the Ford and wait for me, and then I'd head back for Boston."

"Somebody said something about some money," the kid said.

"If I was you," Dillon said, "I'd look hard for that convertible. You drive that convertible back to Boston and let me off and if I was you I'd look in that glove compartment for about a thousand bucks before I dropped that car off in the nigger district."

"Is it gonna be hot?" the kid said.

"Does a bear shit in the woods?" Dillon said.

The traffic thinned out rapidly when they got across the river into Cambridge. They proceeded north, following the Route 91 signs. Three miles onto 91 north, they were hitting sixty-five. "You're gonna turn off pretty soon here," Dillon said.

"I know, I know," the kid said.

When the Ford was alone on the road, Dillon

brought the revolver up and held it an inch behind Coyle's head, the muzzle pointing at the base of the skull behind the left ear. Dillon drew the hammer back. The first shot went in nicely. Dillon continued firing, double-action. The revolver clicked on a spent round at last. Coyle lay thrust up against the frame between the doors of the Ford. The speedometer read eighty-five.

"Slow down, you stupid shit," Dillon said. "You want to get arrested or something?"

"I got nervous," the kid said. "There were so many of them."

"There was nine of them," Dillon said. The car stank of gunpowder.

"It was loud in here," the kid said.

"That's why I use a twenty-two," Dillon said. "I ever let off a thirty-eight two-incher in here, you'd've gone right off the road."

"Is he dead?" the kid said.

"If he isn't," Dillon said, "he's never gonna be. Now slow down and get off this road."

The bowling alley was dark. The kid pulled the sedan in next to the Ford convertible. "Hey," he said, "that looks a lot like this car, in this light."

"You're learning," Dillon said, "that's the idea. Cops've been seeing that car all night. Now they're gonna see another one that looks almost just like it. They won't search it for a couple hours. Help me stuff him down there."

They crammed Coyle down onto the floor of the right passenger compartment. They got out of the Ford. "Lock it," Dillon said. "Keeps the volunteers out of it."

They got into the convertible. It started at once. "Not a bad car," the kid said.

"Not a bad car at all," Dillon said. "Now go back Memorial Drive and take the Mass. Ave. bridge, I gotta get rid of this gun."

30

JACKIE BROWN at twenty-seven sat with no expression on his face in the first row behind the bar of Courtroom Four of the United States District Court for the District of Massachusetts.

The clerk called case number seventy-four-hundred-and-twenty-one-D, United States of America versus Jackie Brown. The bailiff motioned to Jackie Brown to rise.

Also rising was a man beyond the bar. "The case is called for arraignment, your honor," he said. "The defendant is present with counsel."

The clerk said: "Jackie Brown, you are charged in this indictment with five counts of possessing machine-guns which were not registered to you in the National Firearms Transfer and Registration Record. What say you to this indictment, are you guilty or not guilty?"

Getting up now, slowly, was Foster Clark, counsel for the defendant. "Not guilty," he said in a hoarse whisper.

Jackie Brown looked at Foster Clark contemptuously. "Not guilty," he said.

"Bail," the judge said.

"The defendant is free in ten thousand dollars personal security," the prosecutor said. "The government recommends the same bail be continued."

"Any objection?" the judge said.

"None," Foster Clark said.

"Is this case ready for trial?" the judge said.

"The government is ready for trial," the prosecutor said.

"The defendant," Foster Clark said, "the defendant would like twenty days to file special pleas."

"Motion allowed," the judge said. He consulted his calendar. "This case will be tried on January sixth. How long does the government anticipate the trial will take?"

"We have nine witnesses," the prosecutor said. "Two days, perhaps two and a half."

"We will be in recess," the judge said.

In the corridor outside Courtroom Four, Foster Clark approached the prosecutor. "I was wondering," he said, "are we really going to have to try this case?"

"Well," the prosecutor said, "that depends. He's dead on and gone to heaven, if that's what you mean. He doesn't have a prayer."

"I was wondering if we could work something out," Clark said. "I haven't really had a chance to talk with him, but I was wondering."

"So talk to him," the prosecutor said. "Find out where he stands, and call me."

"Suppose he talks," Clark said, "what're you going to recommend?"

"Look," the prosecutor said, "you know I can't answer that. I never know for sure what the boss is going to want me to do. So why kid each other. My guess, my guess would be we ask for some jail if he pleads, and a lot of jail if he doesn't."

"Good Christ," Clark said, "you guys want to put the world in jail. This is a young kid. He doesn't have a record. He didn't try to hurt anybody. He's never been

in court before in his life. He doesn't even have a goddamned traffic ticket, for God's sake."

"I know that," the prosecutor said. "I also know he
was driving a car that cost four grand and he's twenty-
seven years old and we can't find a place he ever
worked. He's a nice, clean-cut gun dealer, is what he is,
and if he wanted to, he could probably make half the
hoods and forty per cent of the bikies in this district.
But he doesn't want to do that. Okay, he's a stand-up
guy. Stand-up guys do time."

"So he's got to talk," Clark said.

"Nope," the prosecutor said, "he doesn't have to do a
damned thing except decide which he wants to do
more, talk, and make somebody important for us, or go
down to Danbury there and get rehabilitated."

"That's a pretty tough choice to make," Clark said.

"He's a pretty tough kid," the prosecutor said. "Look,
we don't need to stand here and play the waltz music.
You know what you got: you got a mean kid. He's been
lucky up to now; he's never been caught before. And
you know what I got, too: I got him fat. You've talked
to him. You saw him and you told him it was talk or
take the fall, and he told you to go and fuck yourself, or
something equally polite. So now you got to try the
case, because he won't plead without a deal that puts
him on the street and I don't make that kind of deal for
machinegun salesmen that don't want to give me anything. So we try this one, and it'll take two days or so,
and he'll get convicted. Then the boss'll tell me to say
three, or maybe five, and the judge'll give him two, or
maybe three, and you'll appeal, maybe, and some time
around Washington's Birthday, he'll surrender to the
marshals and go down to Danbury for a while. Hell,

he'll be out in a year, year and a half. It isn't as though he was up against a twenty-year minimum mandatory."

"And in another year or so," Clark said, "he'll be in again, here or someplace else, and I'll be talking to some other bastard, or maybe even you again, and we'll try another one and he'll go away again. Is there any end to this shit? Does anything ever change in this racket?"

"Hey Foss," the prosecutor said, taking Clark by the arm, "of course it changes. Don't take it so hard. Some of us die, the rest of us get older, new guys come along, old guys disappear. It changes every day."

"It's hard to notice, though," Clark said.

"It is," the prosecutor said, "it certainly is."